I0624778

♥ Sweet haven ♥

JP SAYLE

Copyright © 2021 by JP Sayle

All rights reserved. No part of this publication may be reproduced, distributed, or transmitted in any form or by any means, including photocopying, recording, or other electronic or mechanical methods, without the prior written permission of the publisher, except in the case of brief quotations embodied in critical reviews and certain other noncommercial uses permitted by copyright law.

Book Cover © 2021 Design by Tina Løwén
People in images are models and should not be connected to the characters in the book. Any resemblance is incidental.

Editing by HL Day
Proofreading by HL Day
Book Formatting by Tina Løwén

References to real people, events, organisations, locations, or establishments are only intended to give a sense of authenticity and have been used fictitiously.

The author acknowledges the copyrighted or trademarked status and trademark on Kalvin Cline.

Films, music, and lyrics mentioned are the property of the copyright holders.

Warning
Some of the content of this book is sexually graphic, with the use of explicit language and adult situations involving two males. It is only intended for mature audiences.

Books By The Author

Ferron's Journey: Revelation Part Three #6

Mine, Body and Soul Trilogy

Ferron's Journey Trilogy

Dark River Stone Collective Series

The Light Beneath the Dark #1

The Billionaire Playground Series

Property of a Billionaire #1

Reluctant Billionaire #2

The Manx Cat Guardians Series

Where it all Began: Origins #1

Seeing Beyond the Scars #2

Destiny Collides Past and Present #3

Searching for a Soul to Love #4

The 12 Disasters of Christmas #5

Laws of Attraction #6

The Teacher's Boy #7

Boxset

Audio Books

Mine, Body and Soul, Part One

Mine, Body and Soul, Part Two

Mine, Body and Soul, Part Three

Daddy Kink: The App (book one)

Always More: The Flamingo Bar

When Fake Changed Everything

Ferron's Journey: Damaged Part One

Ferron's Journey: Hidden Part Two

Ferron's Journey: Revelation Part Three

Story Outline

A grumpy chef, a klutz, an ad for an assistant and a sister who has no boundaries. Are these the perfect ingredients for love?

Confectionery chef, Garrett Weston returns to his hometown to lick his wounds after his marriage fails. His sister encourages him to open a confectionery store, but then throws a spanner in the works leaving him in need of a new assistant.

Leeson Cole moves to Sweet Haven to escape past mistakes. He's been saving every cent he has to fulfil a lifelong ambition of working in the confectionery business. The job at Sweet Haven's store seems like a dream come true. All Leeson needs to do is hope his klutzy behavior doesn't ruin things for him before he has a chance to prove he's got what it takes. *Easy.*

Sweet Haven is a steamy standalone, opposites attract MM romance, with a grumpy bear and a not so delicate flower who can create chaos out of nothing, finding their HEA.

It takes many steps to complete a book and I wouldn't be able to this wonderful job without the help of Julie, HL, Tina, Mandy and Robert. Much love!

Garrett

I placed the chocolate I'd pulled out of the refrigerator on the counter and stared at my sister. She'd come in dressed in her usual skinny jeans and T-shirt with the logo of the store on it. All that was missing was her apron. Her blonde curls were tied up in a bun on top of her head, her freckled face devoid of make-up demonstrating flawless skin despite her appalling diet that she bragged about all the damn time. "How can you be heading to Los Angeles? I've only just returned home."

"Big brother, you've been back several months, and you only came back to lick your wounds after that dick of a husband decided he didn't want to compete with a top chef anymore."

"Let's leave Teddy out of this for now. I don't want to think about him. What I do want to know is how I'm supposed to run the store *and* make all the confectionery I'm supposed to be so famous for?"

Her eye roll and head shake were to be expected when the last thing I wanted to talk about, was her leaving to go and pursue her own dreams.

"There is such a thing as running an ad for an assistant."

I held my hand up, already getting a headache at the thought of having to interview people who knew nothing about my business, or how to entice customers to buy sweet things when half the town always seemed to be on a goddamn diet.

Returning to my hometown, Sweet Haven, had seemed like a good idea at the time. Opening a confectionery store had seemed like an even better idea. Only that one hadn't been mine. It had been my sister's idea, and now she was looking to leave just when things were finally starting to take off. Sweet Haven wasn't the most forward thinking of towns when it came to stores with fancy candy and chocolates. Initially, it had seemed like a step too far for the town's inhabitants.

During the first month of opening, I'd had the grand total of ten folk through the door. The thousands of dollars I'd ploughed into buying the store, along with the renovations needed to make it look perfect, had seemed a total waste. In Los Angeles I'd been the king of confection and there'd been queues outside the door to buy the things I sold. Whereas here, they could barely be bothered to try. I'd persevered though, because it was what I did. Teddy was living proof of that. When he'd given up on our marriage, consumed by an ugly jealousy at my success, I'd still tried to work at it.

My shoulders sagged, my sister's fingers snapping in front of my face. I blinked my sister back into focus. "Sorry, were you saying something?"

"Don't give me that bullshit. You know I was. Let me sort out an ad and do the interviews for you. I know how picky you are, and I can't afford to wait ten years for you to make a decision."

I gave a sheepish smile. "Hey, I'm not that bad."

There was a look of disbelief on her face as she stared at me. "Yes, you are. How long did it take to pick out the range in the kitchen? I'll tell you how long—six months! Who takes six months just to pick something to cook on? Then there were the refrigerators and the coolers."

Seeing she was building up quite a head of steam that showed no sign of disappearing, I side-stepped around the counter, picking up a spiced chocolate and then pushing it between her parted lips.

"Oh… my… just wow," she mumbled around the chocolate before shutting her eyes and starting to groan like… well, I didn't want to think about what the sounds were like, not when they were coming from my sister. That was just yuck!

"Now I can get a word in edgeways."

It was her turn to hold up her hand while she kept her eyes closed. "Chili, ginger, and a hint of something spicy that I can't quite pinpoint." Her eyes, a bold blue just like mine, opened to show her appreciation. It gave me the same warm feeling it always did when someone showed enjoyment of the taste explosion in their mouth. It made all the time and effort worthwhile. "Yep, you nailed it. What's the spice?" She eyed the counter where several more samples were laid out.

At some ungodly hour in the morning, I'd woken with the idea in my head. Once the urge to create had struck, I was doomed until I'd figured out the new recipe. "Take one step closer to those chocolates, and I'll—"

"You'll what? Wrestle me to the floor?"

We'd wrestled before, and she was a sneaky fucker when it came to getting her own way. There was a gleam in her eyes that had me stepping in front of her, because I knew damn well she'd risk life and limb for my chocolate. "If I have to. These"—I pointed vaguely toward where the tray sat on the counter— "are to put out on the counter to get some feedback."

Teasing the customers with new tastes they didn't need to pay for was how I'd eventually managed to build my business up. It had also been a great way of figuring out what to focus on selling in the store.

The online business Jen had insisted on me starting to see if I could entice my old customers to buy online was showing signs of making a profit after just two months. It was all great, as long as I didn't think about my sister leaving me high and dry just when my life was returning to some sort of normality. My sister said that I was hiding. I disagreed. I was just giving myself some breathing room after being stabbed in the back by my husband. *Correction—my soon to be ex-husband!*

"Why are you scowling at me like that?"

"I was thinking about Teddy. I... got the paperwork to finalize the divorce." Although I didn't have feelings for Teddy anymore, it was the thought of it being so final. It would be the end of an era, and of all the dreams I used to hope of building with Teddy.

Jen approached me, wrapping her arms around my waist and laying her blonde head against my chest, her bun tickling the underside of my chin. "He's an asshole, and he isn't worth spitting on."

I chuckled and hugged her back. "I know. But it wasn't just him. I've had plenty of time to reflect on how we grew apart. The more successful I got, the bigger the gap between us became. In the end both of us were to blame for our failed marriage. I put so much of myself into building up the business that I forgot I needed to do the same for my relationship. What have I got left, apart from a wad of cash? It just feels wrong."

"Nonsense, you walked away because he stole from you, and he didn't want to work on your relationship. He never did, not even at the beginning. You've come home and proved that it was you who made the business a success, not him. Your amazing creativity is off the charts, and the townsfolk are seeing that, as are the people in the neighboring towns. Word is getting out, and business is thriving. When your old customers discover you're doing a delivery service, you'll be inundated with so many orders you won't know what to do with yourself. Now all you need is the right man."

I patted her back as her body vibrated with an enthusiasm that was hard to ignore. "Don't wish that on me. Men are off limits, and I would like to be able to get some sleep sometimes. Let's hope for only as much work as I can cope with."

"What you need, is to get a life! You haven't been out on one date since you came back. Not one!" She glared at me as if she knew I was about to dispute the fact. "Bill, or whatever his name was, doesn't count, because you dated him in high school. And you didn't even kiss him."

Cheeks heated, I released her and swung around to face the counter. I hated talking about my sex life, but she seemed to have no such issues with wanting all the details. "Let it go. There was no attraction between us. I realized it the minute I accepted his offer. It was more about talking about old times. I told you that."

"There must be a nice gay guy in town for you."

I didn't need to see her face to know there would be a glint of mischief in her eyes, her voice giving her away. "That right there is a no, Jen. You hear me?" I collected the dirty bowls and walked over to the sink, hoping the conversation about my lack of love-life would, like the topic of Teddy had, be dropped. The thing was, my sister wasn't one for letting anything drop once she'd gotten it into her head that she could help me.

Placing the dirty dishes in the sink, I turned on the faucet while I tried to come up with something to distract her. "Put out an ad then for an assistant." I glanced back over my shoulder at her. "Just make sure you're clear about the early starts and how much work is involved."

"Of course." A smile spread across her pretty face, her dimples deepening and making my stomach tighten. "I know exactly what you need. Leave it to me."

"Famous last words," I muttered as I looked down at the pans. *If there's a God listening up there, make sure she doesn't land me with a dud!*

1
Leeson

"OMG! Have you seen this ad for an assistant at Sweet Haven's Confectionery store?" Ollie said with a squeal as I entered the two-bed apartment we'd shared since moving to Sweet Haven to escape our pasts, two years earlier.

His words scarcely registered through the fatigue that felt all consuming. "How can I have seen it? I've just walked through the door, and I've been at the diner all day. It's not like Ed lets me have any more time than it takes to use the bathroom. You know that man is a slave driver!" I rolled my aching shoulders back as I dragged my weary ass over to the sagging sofa and collapsed in a relieved heap.

There was barely enough energy left inside me to carry me across the room to see what Ollie was waving at me, my brain mush after a fourteen-hour day. With Ollie currently injured, we needed the money to pay the rent and survive. He was a tad bit clumsy, as was I, but he was the one who'd fallen down a flight of stairs and broken his ankle leaving me with all the bills to pay.

"I'm sorry. You know I'll pay you back as soon as I'm on my feet again. It should hopefully only be another month. Richard has said he'll keep my job in the art store open.

He's struggling without me, but he's going to wait till my leg is healed."

His voice was thick with emotion, so I swallowed a sigh, refusing to think about another month of back-breaking fourteen-hour days. "Don't stress, I'll survive." I lifted my arm and flexed my biceps to make the muscle pop through my thin T-shirt. "I'll be buff and irresistible by the time I'm finished."

A whiff of grease wafted up as I dropped my arm. I sniffed, the scent of grease and stale coffee making my nose wrinkle. "If I can get the smell of grease off me that is. I smell worse than last week's congealed fat that I had to clean out of the fat fryer Ed seems to use for everything he cooks."

Ollie hobbled across the floor, his crutches scraping the wood. He sat next to me, the compression of the cushion making me roll toward him. Too tired to stop myself, I lay my head on his shoulder. "Give me five, and then I'll get up and make us something to eat."

"I made a chili. It won't be up to your standards, but it will be edible," Ollie stated as he patted my arm.

"You're a lifesaver. Now all I need is the energy to go and heat it up." I really didn't have the energy to move, but I'd not eaten for eight hours, and my stomach was beginning to think my throat had been cut with all the loud gurgling noises coming from it.

Ollie rolled forward, his rotund body making the sofa cushions tilt. I toppled into him as he struggled to stand on his good leg. A huff came from Ollie as I grunted from the impact, too tired to right myself.

"I can't give you a piggyback. You know that, right?" He giggled as he shifted, shoving me away before standing.

My breath caught in my throat as he wobbled before he managed to right himself and get his crutches to hold his weight. "I think you could. Those metal crutches look sturdy enough."

He cast me a sideways glance and shook his head. "They struggle to hold my weight." He waved the crutch around with his left arm as if he was trying to dance, drawing my gaze to his rounded middle. "This isn't a body made for athletics. It's more for sofa surfing." His tone was resigned and I got up off the sofa, my weariness forgotten in my need to set him straight.

His ex-boyfriend had given him a complex about his weight by talking about it constantly, to the point where he wouldn't even roam around the apartment without a T-shirt on. I took hold of his forearms and looked him dead in the eye so he knew how serious I was. "There is nothing wrong with your body. Nothing. Your ex was a freak. Who wants to be a string bean with no nice parts to hold on to? That's no one's idea of hot, I'm telling you."

His cheeks turned a deep shade of red as his gaze lowered to his midsection. "I'm fat. I accept that. I don't have the energy or inclination to change it, so I'll stay single and just accept it."

"Fuck that! Granted, you've got a little extra timber around your middle, but you've been immobile for weeks, and once the plaster comes off, you can do

21

something about it. Or you can just embrace it and become the male Lizzo, who I might add is as fit as fuck, even though she's a girl."

"I could so channel Lizzo," Ollie said with an enthusiasm that had been missing before.

I grinned at him. "Then stop calling yourself fat because you're being demeaning to yourself and it's insulting. I love you. I've loved you since kindergarten. You're a beautiful person inside and out." I gave him a gentle shake. "All negative language about weight in this apartment is banned from now on."

He took a shuddery breath, and then another, before finally answering. "Okay. I'll try."

"Nope, you ain't trying. You're going to do it and that's the end of it."

"You're so bossy," Ollie muttered, but his lips were twitching as I let him go.

"Yes, I am. But when have I ever been any different?" Ollie's lips parted and I shook my head. "Nope, don't even mention Snake Breath. Mention of him is also banned from the apartment."

"Does that mean I can mention him when we're not in here?" Ollie called after me as I headed to the small kitchen to reheat the chili.

Without stopping, I shouted back, "Only if you want me to stop making you the treats you hide in your bedroom."

There was a choked cough, a memory niggling its way to the surface. I paused in the doorway of the kitchen to look back at Ollie. "What was it you said about Sweet Haven needing an assistant?" My heart rate picked up as his face lit up with the biggest smile, turning him from cute to stunning.

"Your favorite chef is advertising for an assistant."

"Are you shitting me?" All thoughts of the meal were forgotten as I walked back over to Ollie, his grin growing wider.

"Would I lie to you?"

My heart fluttered wildly in my chest as I stared at Ollie. "Tell me everything you know."

2

Garrett

The scent of spice and warm chocolate filled the air as I attempted to improve on the chocolate samples that had flown off the counter. A chuckle rose as I recalled what had had happened earlier to Ollie, one of my best customers. In his haste to get to the counter to get to the freebies first, he'd nearly fallen off his crutches, risking giving himself another injury.

Folks in town had been out in force today. It was almost as if someone had gone to the main store and told everyone I'd be behind the counter. They'd all seemed to want to catch up and say "hi." A shudder ran through me as I tried not to think about all the hours I'd spent avoiding nosey questions while Jen had carried out the interviews. After the morning in the store, I'd decided that she'd gotten the better deal. Although, for all I knew, the applicants could all have been total timewasters.

She hadn't let me see the applications, informing me that I'd only pick holes in everyone. She wasn't wrong, but we were on a countdown to her leaving, and I needed her to train a replacement. Not that I held out much hope of her finding what I needed in these parts.

The last thing I needed was to be left training some idiot on how to use the cash register, or how to package the candy to make it look presentable in the specially chosen boxes.

Sniffing the pot, I picked up a star anise pod and dropped it into the warm liquid to see if it would add another level to the flavor. Stirring the thick, dark chocolate, I kept one eye on the thermometer to ensure it didn't burn. My mother said I'd only had one interest as a child, and that was in making things people could eat. That passion had stayed with me, my parents using some of their retirement fund to send me to train with top confectioners in Paris once I'd decided that was what I wanted to do. That had been twenty years ago, and I'd more than paid back the money so that they could fulfil their own dreams of buying a condo and retiring to Florida.

Does money make you happy?

It hadn't been enough to save my marriage. I absently stirred the pot, considering whether if I'd come back here with all my sparkly new certificates and awards from Paris, things would have been different between me and Teddy.

My chuckle sounded anything but humorous at the thought of Teddy in Sweet Haven—population eighty-five thousand. Quite simply, he'd have hated it. When I'd met him in Paris, our mutual passion for cooking had provided an instant attraction. Well, that and the fact he was easy on the eye. He'd been training to be a chef, his specialty the same as mine—confectionery. I'd been blinded by how perfect we were together.

The only thing was, that he'd lacked the flair in the kitchen that seemed to come naturally to me. I'd been so caught up in my need to show the world what I could do, that I'd raced ahead, not noticing that the more successful I became, the more withdrawn Teddy became. I could see it now when I looked back. With every new award our confectionery business had achieved, my self-importance had grown. All my attention had been so focused on making our joint business a success that I'd lost sight of what was happening between us.

We'd gotten married as it had felt like the next step, but then Teddy had decided to leave me to the business, so that he could focus on... Well, I wasn't sure what he'd focused on besides taking everything I had to give. I'd given Teddy whatever his heart desired, including a mansion in LA's most popular area, and a top designer to kit it out. I'd indulged him because we were in love, or so I'd thought. It had turned out that he was more in love with my credit card, and the expensive lifestyle I provided while he worked on his tan beside the pool at our mansion. Had I been at fault for not seeing that he'd been struggling with my success?

Stop it, you did your best.

Had I? Or had I given him money so that I could hide from what had been happening between us? I shook off the same questions that had plagued me ever since the divorce papers had arrived the week before. All the self-recrimination in the world wouldn't change the fact he'd sold the business behind my back, conning me into signing a form while I'd been distracted after yet another fight.

The scent of burning chocolate met my nose and I cursed as I lifted the pot off the heat. I swung around, my lips parting in surprise as I met a pair of bright emerald eyes. Eyes, that seemed to dominate the whole of the guy's gorgeous face. My heart rate picked up, but I put it down to the fright of finding someone in my kitchen. "Who are you and what are you doing in my kitchen?"

"Hi, I'm Lee. Jen said to come straight back and introduce myself." Lee eyed my hand, his eyebrows rising and his nose wrinkling. "Smells like you burnt the chocolate."

He sounded so disappointed that I scowled at him. "What business is it of yours?"

A slash of deep red highlighted the guy's cheekbones. "I erm, well, I... You see... I..."

"Spit it out. It's not like I have all day for you to say what's on your mind," I growled, feeling a little put out, the odd sensation leaving me confused as the guy dipped his gaze and toed at the tiled floor.

"I'm your new assistant," he mumbled so quietly that I had to strain to hear him.

"You're shitting me." My gaze raked over him from head to toe. What the fuck was my sister playing at? This guy barely looked strong enough to survive a gust of wind. His features were delicate, and he looked... well, fragile.

I didn't need a fragile guy who would probably quit after one day of working in the store. I groaned, rolling my eyes to the ceiling. Once I'd gotten rid of this guy, I was going to kill Jen.

"Listen, I'm sure you think you know what goes on in a confectionery kitchen." My gaze swept over him again, taking in his willowy body clad in scruffy jeans and a T-shirt that looked like it had seen better days. "This place isn't for weaklings."

Deep furrows appeared around his eyes and I increased my initial estimation of his age from eighteen to mid-twenties, which was still a lot younger than my forty-one years.

"Excuse me, I'm no weakling. I bet I could run rings around you in your"—his arm swept the room—"fancy pants kitchen."

I bristled at the description of my no-expense-spared kitchen. "This is a working kitchen required for someone of my skill to be creative," I ground out through gritted teeth, hating how pompous I was coming across.

His lips pursed, his gaze traveling to the hand still holding the pot of burnt chocolate. Heat spread up my neck, and it took a lot of effort to control the urge to throw it in the sink. I thought I'd outgrown the temper tantrums I'd been famous for in some circles.

As I waited for the little upstart to say what was clearly on his mind, my grip on the handle of the pot increased until my knuckles turned white. The guy barely reached the middle of my chest. At six-foot-four, most men had to look up to meet my gaze, but even though this guy was a foot shorter than me, the way he looked at me felt as if he was looking down on me.

"If you're all that, then how did you burn the chocolate? Your sister raved about how fantastic you are in the kitchen. Seems she was wrong."

My mouth opened and then closed again. I was at a total loss as to how to respond. I couldn't recall the last time someone had had the audacity to speak back to me, never mind to point out an error, which in my defence very rarely happened.

A pounding grew in my ears as I slowly walked over to the counter that cut the kitchen in half to place the pot down on the stainless-steel. I rested my hands on the counter so that I didn't reach out and grab the scrawny guy's throat, enunciating every word, "Get out of my kitchen! Now."

Less than two seconds later, my sister appeared in the open doorway, her carefully shaped eyebrows hidden by her bangs. She gave me a furious stare as she stepped fully into the kitchen. "Do you want to explain to me why the main street can hear you shouting?"

A slick of sweat coated my palms as I glared at her. "Ask whatever his name is."

"My name's Leeson, and all I did was point out that you burnt the chocolate. What kind of professional are you that can't manage to keep a check on the temperature?"

Steam all but coming out of my ears, I moved swiftly around the counter, my sister exhaling sharply. She stepped in front of Leeson, her hands coming up, as if that would stop me from wringing the fucker's neck for daring to criticize my cooking skills.

"Get out of my way, Sis."

Jen took one look at my face and pressed her hands against my chest, shaking her head. "Not happening. What was it you said about having outgrown your temper tantrums? Leeson only pointed out the obvious." She glanced back to the counter where the offending chocolate sat, sniffing the air, her expression demonstrating that she couldn't detect the slightly acrid scent. Her nose wasn't as good as mine, or apparently Leeson's. "Did you burn the chocolate?" she demanded in a tone that said she wasn't up for any bullshit.

The urge to lie was strong as Leeson's face appeared around Jen's shoulder, daring me to say differently. "Yes." I all but spat at her. The look of surprise that crossed her face would have been comical were it not for the man behind her grinning like a cat that had eaten all the cream. Smug fucker!

"Holy crap! I had a good feeling about Leeson and this proves it." Jen dropped her hands from my chest, turning her back to me to hug Leeson hard enough that he squealed loudly.

Served him right.

"You're perfect," said Jen.

"What, wait… No, he's not," I muttered. Jen ignored me, guiding Leeson toward the tiny office housed in what used to be a large storage room.

I had to shout after her. "What are you doing?"

She didn't look back, my heart sinking as she called back, "Finalising Leeson's paperwork."

"I told you, I don't…" I stopped talking as the office door slammed shut, realizing I was wasting my breath.

I stood like a damn fool, staring down the hallway. What was I going to do now? Wait until she left for LA and then fire him? Nope, I'd work him so hard that he quit. A smile settled on my face as the idea took root.

Yeah, that would work. It had worked in the past.

3
Leeson

The second the door banged shut behind me, my legs started to shake. I was sure Jen must be able to hear the bones rattling together as I stumbled toward the chair in front of the tiny office desk. The second my ass hit the leather seat, I buried my head between my knees, hoping some sense would return along with the blood that had been pooling in my lap ever since the grumpy fucker in the kitchen had turned to face me and growled. God, I was a sucker for a big, grumpy dude.

Why did he have to be everything I loved?

Why?

Those eyes of his... Jeez, they should be outlawed. The blue was crystal clear, like the water surrounding the Maldives. They were eyes that seemed to reach inside me and find all my hidden secrets. Shit, all I'd wanted was to drown in those eyes. Or at least I had until he'd opened his mouth. I groaned, recalling the verbal diarrhea that had quite literally poured out of me. *Why didn't I come with an off switch?* Ollie often said that my mouth worked faster than my brain. Today, I'd more than proved him right. The only saving grace was that I'd taken a sick day from the diner instead of quitting, so I still had a job.

"You aren't going to puke or anything, are you?" Jen asked. I shook my head without risking looking up, Jen sounding a little more relaxed as she continued, "That's good, because there's no way I can clean up puke. You can stop hiding. I'm sure my brother won't follow us. He's in too much of a temper right now, to do much more than stomp around the kitchen and throw shit."

I chanced looking up. If I'd expected her to be pissed at the way I'd spoken to her brother, then I was wrong. If anything, she looked amused. Her dimples winked at me as she perched on the edge of the desk, her legs swinging back and forth as if she had too much energy to sit still.

"I'm so sorry for... well, calling your brother out like that–"

"Nonsense! The stuffed shirt needs someone to stand up to him. You've got nothing to apologize for. He burnt the chocolate. The fact you knew that, shows that you didn't lie to me, and proves I have the skills to pick my brother a partner."

I gulped, my tongue stuck to the roof of my mouth. "Say what?"

Jen continued to grin at me like I was some sort of prize she'd won at the fairground. "Partner, you know, a person who works with another person to build a business." Even as she spoke, I got a strange sense that that wasn't exactly what she'd meant. The fact my pulse had skipped excitedly was totally not the point. *It wasn't!*

The guy in the kitchen was a total fox with his dark brown hair flecked with silver. Slashing cheekbones, bold blue eyes, and lips that were fuller and riper than any peach I'd ever eaten completed the picture. I could also wax lyrical about his broad shoulders and massive barrel chest that made me wonder if it was covered in hair. The blood that had returned to my head, decided to head back south, and I tried to recall the last time I'd felt this level of arousal. The obvious answer was never. Did it make me a sadist that no matter how grumpy the guy had been, I still found him attractive?

The answer made me cringe. *Oh, I was in so much trouble.* I should refuse the job, go back to the diner, and forget I'd ever applied for the stupid job in the first place. That wasn't what came out of my mouth, though. "Where's the paperwork you want me to fill in?"

I refused to acknowledge the gleam of satisfaction in Jen's eyes, or the knots forming in my stomach at the thought of spending more time getting the famous Garrett Weston riled up. I'd been following his career way before Ollie and I had arrived in town. It was only when someone had mentioned his name and the fact he'd been born here that I'd gone all stalkerish, searching out pictures on the internet. They hadn't done him justice. Ollie knew all about my obsession with Garrett's career, and how I wanted to emulate it, but now my obsession was going to take a turn that I wasn't sure I was prepared for.

Jen twisted around, her gaze traveling over the desk. She stood and heaved out a breath. "Why does he have to be such a neat freak in here, but a slob in the kitchen?"

I had no answer, waiting for her to find what Garrett must have tidied away.

"Aha, here we go." She pulled a stack of papers out of a drawer and placed them next to me. "Can you fill in all your details? Then I'll need your clothes size, so that I can supply you with both kitchen and store wear. It can get messy in the kitchen, so I tend to keep a couple of sets of clothing here. Garrett lives in the apartment above the store. I normally shower up there if I get too sweaty before heading into the store to run the counter. I'm sure he won't mind you using his spare bathroom."

She continued to talk as I filled out the forms. I chose not to argue about her brother being keen on me stepping into his home after his reaction to me being in his kitchen. *You did point out that he'd fucked up his chocolate by letting it burn. Yeah, well. I thought he was the top honcho of confectionery.*

The silent argument in my head continued and I lost track of what Jen was saying. It was only as she said, "will that be fine with you?" that I clued in to having missed something important.

I gave her my most winning smile as I looked up. "I was concentrating on the forms. Sorry, I missed the last part of what you said."

"I was checking that you'll be fine to start next week? I'll need time to show you everything before I head off for the bright lights and big city." Her smile lit up the room.

Her excitement was catching, and I found myself matching her smile, keeping the questions I had about what her plans were to myself. "I'll need to give Ed a weeks' notice. Is that okay? I don't want to leave him in the lurch. He's been good to me." *Well, he'd given me extra hours.*

She nodded. "That's fine. I've known Ed all my life. He's a cantankerous old bastard, but I wouldn't want you to leave him shorthanded. I'm sure he'll fill your position quickly. Okay, I take that back. The towns folk all know him so it might take more than a week," she said with a chuckle.

Once all the details were sorted and the paperwork completed, I braced myself to leave the office and return to the kitchen. *Keep your mouth shut. Whatever you do, keep your lips buttoned.*

I kept that thought on repeat as Jen ushered me back down the hallway and into the kitchen to where a grumpy-faced Garrett stood at the counter making no effort to look in our direction.

"I'm going to show Lee around." Jen glanced at me. "You go by Lee or Leeson?"

"Lee," Garrett muttered before I could answer.

I bit my lower lip at the obvious olive branch he was offering by remembering how I'd introduced myself before it had all gone to hell in a hand cart. I stayed silent as Jen grinned at me. "Lee, it is then. I'll be giving Lee a key to the apartment so that he can use my room to store some spare clothes in, in case of emergencies."

Garrett mumbled something I didn't quite catch. Jen must have though, because her dimples winked to life and there was a suspicious light in her eyes that caused my nerves to hum to life. What was she up to?

I wasn't given a chance to figure it out as I was ushered out of the kitchen and back through the closed store. Jen had already gone through how the day normally panned out. Garrett tended to be up at the crack of dawn, and got busy being creative before she arrived around six am to tidy up after him. Then she set up the store with whatever confectionery Garrett had made. The store shut at two pm, and then any online orders were dealt with. Jen had assured me that she was usually finished by three in the afternoon.

It sounded too good to be true. I hadn't worked less than a ten-hour shift in months. Even before Ollie had hurt himself, I'd been working extra hours to save money so that I could eventually take time off to attend a culinary school three towns over.

That was a pipedream at the moment, though, so this would be the next best thing. Or at least it had been until I'd found my hero burning the chocolate. I'd had all these ideals about Garrett, setting him up on a pedestal. And he'd made such a rookie mistake, toppling himself right off of it.

Maybe he had something on his mind and I should stop being so judgemental.

All of the internet research I'd done had said he was getting divorced from his husband of ten years. The pictures I'd found of Teddy showed an elegant man, who looked a little too polished to me. A man that shone that bright usually had no hidden depths in my opinion. *Like you know!*

Closing off the train of thought, I worked to keep my mind on what Jen said as she led me through the store and over to a door I'd paid no attention to earlier when I'd arrived, before she'd encouraged me to go and say hi to Garrett.

I followed her up the cream stairway to the single door at the top.

"He keeps it locked at all times, so remember that when you pop in to use the shower. After living in LA, he's a little anal about people wandering through his home uninvited."

What did she mean when she said "people wandering through his home uninvited?"

The thought fled as the door opened to reveal a large open-plan room. Even if I hadn't already known this was Garrett's home, I would have suspected that whoever owned the place loved to cook just by looking at the focus of the room—the kitchen. It was cream, much like everything else in the room. Only the cream was complemented by forest-green kitchen appliances that gave the space warmth. Green tiles of varying shades, interspersed with cream tiles, covered the wall between the cabinets at the back of the huge kitchen range. My hands itched to touch all the gleaming gadgets just to see what they did.

I'd never been one for fancy things until it came to kitchen appliances. The only thing was that I'd never been able to afford them. My family weren't poor, but they weren't wealthy either. My mother still worked the tills at Walmart and my dad was a motor mechanic. Clothing, feeding, and keeping a roof over the heads of four children had left little for luxuries. Not that any of us had cared. What we'd lacked in possessions my parents had more than made up for with love and affection. They'd always supported us with whatever we wanted from life. That included being on board with which camp my dick preferred.

"As you can see, my brother is more focused on the kitchen than he is on the rest of the apartment."

Pulled from my thoughts by Jen's voice, I glanced in her direction before taking in the rest of the room. The sofas were cream—surprise, surprise, and looked like they were brand new. None of the cushions had an indent to indicate where Garrett preferred to sit. There were a few possessions scattered around the room, but nothing that screamed this is who I am, unlike the kitchen.

A layer of dust covered the large screen TV showing it was rarely used. Everything else though, was dust-free. What did he do during his downtime?

"Garrett lives in the kitchen. His head always seems to be in creative mode."

For a moment I wondered what my expression had revealed. I looked back over to Jen, but she was staring at the kitchen intently. She ran her hands through her hair, dislodging the band that held her hair back so that it tumbled around her face.

As she scraped it back, she said, "I'm hoping you'll give him something else to focus on."

My pulse skipped several beats, my eyes narrowing on her. There was that feeling again. Was she trying to set me up with her brother? No, she wouldn't do that. Would she?

Having only met her twice before, I didn't have a clue what she was capable of, and up to now she'd seemed intent on finding Garrett an assistant to help manage his business.

That's all she means. Stop second guessing her and looking for trouble.

I ignored the sinking sensation in my stomach as Jen pointed in the direction of the hallway. "Let me show which room you can use."

4

Garrett

How had I let my sister talk me into this? How? She was out there now, showing that guy around my store and my home, acting like it was all right. Well, it wasn't all right; it was anything but all right.

For the ten thousandth time, I rolled my eyes to the ceiling, losing track of what I'd been doing, yet again. There was no way I was going to be able to work with the little upstart. And okay, all he'd done was point out that I'd burnt the chocolate. It wasn't a big thing. Only, it was a big thing, and for the life of me I couldn't seem to stop thinking about it.

I was so lost in thought that it took a second to register that Jen had returned without Lee. "Lee's gone. He needs to give a weeks' notice before he can start. His shifts won't allow me to get started on training him until then, so it'll have to wait till next week." She gave a mournful sigh.

I kept my gaze on the pot, giving nothing but a snort in reply.

"Come on, you're being a total grump. You're normally out of it by now. What has got stuck in your craw?"

One glance back over my shoulder was enough to be able to tell she wasn't going to let me ignore her. Her small hands were fisted on her hips and her left foot tapped on the floor, a pink hue covering her face.

"Listen, I'm sure he's a great guy, but he looks like a days' work will kill him."

"Give over, you're never normally one to judge a book by its cover. What's got into you? Was the chocolate comment too much for my famous big brother?"

I could have taken the easy route and just said, yes. Yet I couldn't, not when that meant being stuck with Lee. "He isn't going to be a good fit for me. It's as simple as that. I'll break him, and then you'll get all pissy with me."

"He's not a good fit! Is that right? How the hell would you know when all you did was show how grumpy you are? You didn't ask him what he liked about confectionery. You didn't ask him If he had any interests in this field."

About to challenge her, I stopped when she stomped around the counter to stand in front of me and give me a hard stare. "I'm leaving, big brother, and nothing you can do or say is going to change that. You've had your shot at success. Now it's my turn. I want to make sure you have someone here that shares your passion."

"And you think he does?" I could feel myself losing the argument.

"Yes, I do." She spoke softly, her hand gently touching my arm. The tension riding me had to be obvious from how rigid my arm was. "Give Lee a chance. You'll see he's perfect for you."

"Hang on a minute. Perfect for the store, not for me. That's what you meant, right? Tell me you aren't trying to set me up with... with that guy. Fuck, he barely looks legal."

Her eyelids lowered, leading me to believe for a split second that my suspicions were correct. "Now, would I do that? And for your information he's twenty-nine, so there's only a twelve-year age gap." At the sound of the bell on the front door, Jen swung around, saying nothing more as she walked back out of the kitchen, leaving me brooding.

Was Lee really interested in the business, or was he just after the generous salary we offered? It was a hard question to answer when I hadn't seen his application. I sighed, focusing back on what I was supposed to be doing and shoving Lee to the back of my mind.

The week had flown by, and now that I was faced with the reality that Lee would indeed be working with me, I had a knot of anxiety the size of a football in my stomach. It had also been a week where I'd seemingly lost my mind, because all I could do was think about the guy's pretty face and bright eyes, and the way he'd spoken to me. The more I thought about it, the more worked up I got.

Fuck, it wasn't like me, and that was troubling. So, after sleeping for shit, I'd got up this morning and formulated a plan designed to prove to my sister and Lee that he wasn't cut out for this kind of work.

The kitchen was an unholy mess with crap everywhere and dishes overflowing the sinks. Coming downstairs feeling creative had helped. For the last two hours, I'd been working on some candy with a heart of chocolate for Easter. It could be filled with different flavors which complimented the hard outer shell. I'd had several different pots simmering, which emitted a sweet enough scent to tempt any person intending to abstain from sweet treats. Years of sampling the sweet things while I created them had long since taken the shine off eating them. And I couldn't remember the last time anyone had taken the time to make me a sweet treat.

The sound of the back door opening drew my gaze to the two people stood in the doorway. Lee wore a similar outfit to my sister's: jeans and a loose-fitting chef's jacket with the logo of the store on it in dark blue. She'd picked the colors she liked and it suited her. On Lee, the color was okay. A dark green would probably have make his eyes pop more, though.

Why the fuck are you thinking about which color would bring out his eyes?

You're losing it, stick to the plan!

Lee said nothing, licking his lips nervously as he stood still, his gaze not staying on anything for more than a second. His gaze landed on the sink, his eyes widening. I struggled to keep a smile off my face at his wince. I gave them both a nod and said, "mornin'" before returning my attention to what I'd been doing.

"Right, as you can see my brother is a messy chef. He has no understanding about keeping things to a minimum." Jen's voice carried across the kitchen. "Although today, he seems to have outdone himself."

Heat crept up my neck at her calling me out in front of Lee, and I glared at her. Not that she noticed. She was too busy fussing over Lee. She had this habit of touching people, and I had to bite my lip to stop from telling her to keep her hands to herself.

I've clearly lost all ability to think rationally. I'm like Timothy in Peter Pan. I've lost my marbles. It had to be that. Why else would I be thinking this way?

I listened to Jen's chatter about what happened in the kitchen as she showed Lee where everything was kept. There were several occasions where I tried to add something, but she always beat me to it. By the time they'd reached the sink of dirty dishes, they were both laughing as if they'd been best buddies for years.

"Right, do you want to wash or wipe?"

Expecting him to take the easy option of drying, my eyes widened when Lee answered, "I'll wash." I watched them from the corner of my eye as I went through the motions of making candy.

"Do you have an apron? I can be a bit messy," Lee confessed, sounding more than a little embarrassed.

"Yep, there are several on the back of the door you came through. Go grab one. You might want one of the ones I use though, as Garrett's will be huge on you."

Lee giggled as he walked past me to reach the back door. Not once did he look in my direction which irked me some. "I think my sister's aprons will drown you as well. You're so small," I bit out.

47

He paused three steps from the door to look over in my direction, color rising in his cheeks. "Are you size-ist? You do know that some of the most precious things come in small packages, don't you?" He flounced over to the door, grabbing the first apron to hand before stomping back to join my sister, who stood at the sink with a stupid grin on her face that said "that told you." She remained silent though, as they got to work on the dishes.

Jen never normally shut up so I was used to the noise and chatter, but today was different and it bothered me for some reason. It took a considerable effort not to tell them to keep quiet as I struggled to maintain my concentration.

Two hours later, and with a throbbing head from holding my tongue, the kitchen had been set back to rights. All the dishes had been washed and put away, and the stainless-steel kitchen counters gleamed like a new pin. Lee showed no signs of flagging. In fact, he looked as fresh as a daisy which pissed me off even more for some reason.

Jen pointed to the large bank of coolers and refrigerators that took up the whole of one wall. It was where the confectionery was stored to keep them fresh. "Lee, can you grab the top two trays in the first cooler for me. Then I can show you how to set up the shelves in the store." Jen didn't give him time to answer as she hurried through the door that led into the store.

Lee stood for a few seconds, eyeing the large cooler like it might bite him.

"What's wrong?" I found myself asking when he stayed rooted to the spot.

His gaze didn't shift as he answered, "I'm a little nervous about touching your wonderful confectionery."

The awe in his voice left me so stunned that it took a moment to find my voice. "Well, yes, they are the best candy you'll find in this state."

"Try in the country!" As if embarrassed by what he'd said, Lee marched quickly over to the cooler and yanked the heavy door open with some force. He pressed his back against what I knew to be a cold, heavy door, while he reached for the top two trays. His whole body appeared to judder, my eyes widening as he lurched forward with the trays of candy clutched in his hands.

I roared "watch out," but it was already too late, Leeson losing his grip on one of the trays and all of the candy I'd spent hours making falling to the floor. "For fuck's sake, what are you playing at?" I ranted, running toward him as he attempted to right himself and keep hold of the second tray.

The floor was a colorful array of sugared treats. I could feel them beneath my soles as I grabbed hold of Lee. He started to shake, big fat tears rolling down his pale cheeks.

Snot started to drip out of his nose as he blubbered, "I'm so... sorry... oh, how... mortifying... you're going to sack me... aren't you?"

"Jeez, stop the crying. Go wipe your nose or something." I shoved the trays back in the cooler, trying not to think about the way my stomach twisted from seeing Lee's distressed face. I pushed him gently toward the small washroom, praying that when he returned he'd have stopped snivelling. I couldn't abide folks who cried. Tears made me feel all sorts of out of control and I hated them.

As he disappeared, the door clicking softly shut to block out the sounds of his sobs, Jen came back into the kitchen. She took one look at the mess on the floor and heaved out a huge sigh. "Please tell me you didn't sack him!" she asked, her gaze sweeping the room to find no sign of Lee.

"What did I say about him and this job? I told you he wasn't going to fit in here. The guy has dropped half a tray of candy all over the floor. That's hundreds of dollars wasted. At this rate I'll be bankrupt in a week if he stays." My heart rate spiked as I looked at the mess, and I had to block out the memory of how distressed Lee had been.

"It's not the first time things have been dropped, and it won't be the last. For whatever reason, you're determined not to give him a chance to prove he can do this job standing on his head."

"Maybe if he stood on his head there'd be less chance of him being able to make a mess of my kitchen!"

"I'm sorry. I'll grab my things and I'll pay for what I've wasted. It might take me a while, but I'll pay you back," said Lee, his voice quiet but composed.

Argh, fucking hell!

I swung around to meet Lee's oddly dignified expression, even though his cheeks were blotchy and his eyes were swollen and red-rimmed. The throbbing in my skull had now reached epic proportions, my common sense disappearing along with it. "It's fine. I'm just letting off steam. Clean up the mess, and for now let Jen grab the trays," I gritted out through a clenched jaw. I stomped over to the stove turning off the heat to several of the burners before walking out of the kitchen in search of some pain meds to dull the ache, and hopefully to find my sanity at the same time.

5

Leeson

In the space of three days, all I'd done was make myself look like a total clumsy moron. "Why did I let you talk me into applying for this job? Why? We ain't going to have the money to pay for anything when he kicks me to the curb," I cried mournfully as I sunk deeper into the sofa I'd been sitting on ever since getting home an hour earlier.

"Give over, you're just havin' a few bad days is all."

"Bad days! Bad days are when you wake up after a heavy night boozing it up, and your head feels like it might fall off. The last three days have been so much fucking worse than that. I wanted to die today when I slipped on the floor I'd just mopped. What kind of moron doesn't take care walking on a floor that they'd just wet?" I turned and gave Ollie an accusing look. "Go on, tell me."

When Ollie's eyes gleamed with humour, I grunted, closing my eyes and resting my head back against the cushion.

"What has Jen said?"

"Just that I'm doing great, when clearly I'm not. Garrett's new form of communication with me is to grunt. Not that he spoke much that first day, except to roar at me." I sounded so pathetic that I stopped talking.

"Maybe you're just a little starstruck. Once that settles down, you'll go back to being your normal self."

My eyes opened to slits as I side-eyed my best friend. "Really, you think that's gonna stop me being such a klutz? The two of us could win an award for that. You do know who you're talking to, right? The guy who managed to slip on the only bit of ice in the whole of Sweet Haven and fracture his ass."

Ollie coughed, or possibly choked. It was a close call. I covered my ears to block out the laughter he'd failed to contain.

"Okay, maybe you're a little bit klutzy, but that doesn't mean the guy is gonna sack you."

"I don't have your faith. I'm betting that the second Jen leaves for LA, my feet won't touch the ground he'll have me out that fast. I haven't even had the chance to talk to him about how he comes up with all his ideas," I choked out past a sob. It wasn't even the money. It was the lost opportunity to spend time with someone who I could learn from that made the tears fall.

Ollie placed his arm around my shoulders and tugged me into his body. He kissed the top of my head, groaning, "God, you smell so good."

I gave a watery chuckle, appreciating the fact that he was enjoying the smell that lingered after working in the store rather than hitting on me. Ollie had a sweet tooth to rival any candy lover. His weight gain was mainly because I loved to make candy and chocolates. He was my own personal guinea pig. "You hittin' on me?"

His snort ruffled my hair as he pulled back. "You so aren't my type. I'd break you the moment I bounced on top of you."

"Oh, shut up. You would not."

"Would too," he countered, his voice full of laughter.

My bad mood disappeared as I joined in with his laughter. "How old are you?"

"If you're asking me that, I know you've lost it," he said through his laughter, his shoulders shaking.

"Yeah, yeah, laugh at your poor friend." I gave him a peck on the cheek before I stood, feeling the need to do something to lift my mood. "I think I need to go and be creative."

Ollie's eyes grew wide, his face breaking into a huge smile, a smile that made me wish that life could be that simple. That I could be more than best friends with Ollie because he was such a great guy. We'd never gone there, not once. Somehow, we'd always known that we'd never fit together in that way. Friendship was what worked for us, and I didn't want to lose that for something destined to fail. We both had a type and it clearly wasn't each other. Garrett on the other hand, ticked all of my boxes.

Do not think about Grumpy Pants, don't do it. Even as I repeated it to myself, I knew it was useless when the man was all I could think about. Especially the expression on his face when I'd yet again fucked up and shown him what a disaster I was in his kitchen.

"Whatever has you scowling, forget it, and go find the Lee who can kick creative ass. Make something fucking spectacular and show Mr. Fancy Pants that you're more than just a pretty face."

"You think I'm pretty?" I cooed back, making Ollie roll his eyes at me.

"Nope, you're ugly as sin, but I didn't want to hurt your feelin's. Now go make me candy."

The box I'd tucked into my backpack before leaving the apartment seemed to burn a hole in it, sweat sliding down my back. You can do this, you can. All you need to do is hand over the box and say it's an apology for kicking his shin when you landed in a heap at his feet.

The longer I spent trying to figure out the best way to hand over the box of treats Ollie had raved over, the sweatier I got. By the time I entered through the back of the store, my hoodie was stuck to my back.

"Mornin' sunshine, you're bright and early," Jen said in a jovial tone that matched her smile.

I looked over to where Garrett spent most of his time—at the stove. He didn't so much as glance in my direction. If anything, he seemed to hunch over and do his best to avoid lifting his head.

How was I supposed give him candy when he wouldn't even acknowledge my presence? I swallowed a sigh before it had a chance to escape and slipped my backpack off my shoulder. "Mornin' Jen. After you letting me go a little earlier yesterday, I thought I'd make up the time today." I could have slapped myself for being stupid enough to bring up the day before.

"Hey, you landed hard enough to rattle your bones."

"More like his brain," came the muttered comment from Garrett.

Jen stuck her tongue out at Garrett's back, then winked at me. "How are you feelin' this mornin'? Any sore bits?" Her brows wiggled as she lowered her gaze to my ass.

Convinced the blush I could feel spreading across my face was bright enough to be seen in the dark, I shook my head before hanging up my backpack. I eyed the bag, squaring my shoulders as I reached inside to pull out the small, pink box. The sweet, heavenly scent of mint and rosemary wafted from within it.

Taking a deep inhale designed to stop my heart from leaping from my chest, I walked over to where Garrett stood. "I... you see... I..." The moment Garrett turned those baby blues on me, the spit in my mouth dried up, and I lost the ability to say anything else. I shoved the box into his chest, my fingers brushing against a wall of muscle that left me feeling more than a little breathless.

Oh Gods, could this be any more embarrassing? Seriously, how was I supposed to make a good impression when I acted like a dumb fool around the man?

"What's this?" he growled, his gaze shifting to the box I was squashing against him.

"Something I made. It's an apology for being a... klutz." Pleased I'd managed to string a sentence together, I forgot to let go of the box as Garrett tugged on it.

"Then... are you going to give it to me?"

The question caught me off guard and I answered before I could engage my brain to mouth filter, "Any time you want."

Jen burst out laughing, Garrett's forehead marring with deep furrows. He snatched the box away from me and stepped back. I instantly felt the loss of his body heat, only then realizing how close I'd gotten to him. Was he repelled by the thought of me and him together?

Of course he is. Look at him!

Given that that was the last thing I wanted to do, I chose to focus on Jen. I gave her a sheepish smile, hoping she didn't think I was perving on her brother. I was, totally, but she didn't need to know that.

"Let's get started. Unless you want to wait to see what big brother thinks of your creations?" There was something encouraging about the way she phrased the question. Her eyes gleamed with what looked like mischief as she glanced from me to her brother.

"Erm, no. I'm sure he's too busy to try them now." At the panic in my voice, I wanted the floor to open up and swallow me whole.

But then Garrett spoke. "I'll try them."

Those three words ripped away the prospect of me being long gone when he decided to either throw them away, or to take pity on me and try them. Once Ollie had talked me into taking some for Garrett, I'd been set on "I'll show him." Now I was more on the side of "this is the worst idea ever."

My drying hoodie dampened again as Jen leaned over to peer into the box Garrett was opening. The six chocolates were something I'd been working on for weeks, trying to find the right blend of mint and rosemary that didn't overpower each other or make the chocolate bitter. The coca beans I'd ground to make my own chocolate had cost a small fortune, but I'd wanted to show off so I'd used my stash. What if he hated them?

The sudden realization that his opinion mattered more than I liked, and that he had the power to crush my hopes made the air get stuck in my lungs. Every second that passed as I watched him slowly pick out one of the glossy chocolates, eye it intently, and then lift it to his nose to smell, stretched for so long that I felt like I might pass out before he finally put the chocolate to his lush lips.

I exhaled on a rush, my body twitching as air finally filled my chest. Oh God, oh God, oh God. He's eating my chocolate!

His expression gave absolutely nothing away, but then he let out a kind of moan, or at least I hoped it was that rather than a choking sound, because that wouldn't be good. Was it a moan?

As if Jen sensed my tension, she stuck her hand into the box. She got no further as Garrett slapped at it. "He gave them to me."

The growly tone did all sorts of things to me, reminding me that I was a sick puppy as Jen began to argue. "I'm sure they were meant to be shared?"

She glanced at me, her eyes hopeful. I nodded, not wanting to admit that I'd never given her a second thought when I'd packed the little box.

"See, they're to share." This time, Garrett snatched the box off the counter faster than I could blink. Jen gave a snort of disgust and marched around the counter. "Give me a chocolate," she demanded with her face full of determination.

6

Garrett

Blocking out Jen's constant demands, I stopped her from touching the box, loathe to share the flavor of the chocolate lingering on my tongue with her. Was it only mint and rosemary, or had Lee added something else to the mix? My palate suggested there was another more subtle flavor, but for the life of me I couldn't quite figure out what it was.

Lee watched me like a hawk would its prey, his face showing nothing but concern as he chewed on his lower lip until it looked like it might bleed.

"Garrett, if you don't hand over the box and share, I'm going to..."

"What? Tell Mom on me?" I laughed at her. Due to the fourteen-year age gap between us, this had been her favorite ploy as a child. She'd been an unexpected surprise to my parents. Mom had thought she was going through a phase, instead finding herself with a late pregnancy. As such, Jen had been a spoiled brat and could wrap both our parents around her little finger.

"Don't think I won't ring Mom right now and tell her you're being mean to me." She pointed at me, at the same time reaching for the box. I dodged her grab, lifting the box high so that Jen, who was as short as Lee was, couldn't reach it.

"Are you two always like this?" said Lee in a shocked voice.

Jen and I both looked at him. I could see the disbelief written on his face, but I refused to be embarrassed, battling the heat rising to my cheeks as all Jen did was laugh.

"Yep, I'm spoilt. It comes from being a girl and an extremely late baby. My parents doted on me. What can I say?" She shrugged, walking back over to Lee and wrapping her arm around his waist while batting her eyelashes at him. "You'll make me some chocolate to try too, won't you?"

Lee blushed as he nodded, looking more than a little uncomfortable as he tried to untangle himself from Jen's octopus arms. I'd suspected all along that he was gay. There was something about the way he looked at me when he thought I wasn't paying attention, but this confirmed it. Whenever Jen got all flirty with him, he was clueless how to respond.

"Put him down, Jen. We've got work to be getting on with." As I turned away to put the box of chocolates in my office, I caught Lee's stare. I wasn't sure if I was reading him right, but he looked... disappointed. He had a hangdog expression which wouldn't have been out of place on the beagle we'd had as a child. The dog had had the same look when you went off and left him inside the house. Did Lee want me to give him feedback on the chocolates?

If he did, then he was going to be disappointed as I wasn't quite sure what to say about them. I'd not been expecting much when I'd decided to taste one, but the chocolate hadn't been bitter, and it had had a creamy texture, the glossy shine on its outer shell showing how well the chocolate had been tempered. And if I was honest, all I wanted to do was try another to see if the first had been a fluke, but with Jen and Lee staring at me it would have to wait till I had a moment of privacy.

"Go on, be greedy. Hide those chocolates and don't share. I know Lee will make me a big box next time," Jen shouted at my retreating back.

"Yeah, yeah," I muttered as I walked into my office, searching for a place Jen wouldn't find the box. I checked over my shoulder before placing it on the ledge behind my desk and covering it with a stack of papers. Satisfied Jen wouldn't think to look there, I walked back into the kitchen, trying hard not to think about the effort I'd gone to. They were only chocolates, but they were damn good chocolates, and they were the best I'd tasted in a long time!

Was this what Jen had been alluding to when she'd said that Lee was perfect? Had he mentioned to her that he liked to make confectionery? I needed to check his application. The guy might be the biggest klutz I'd ever encountered, but he had mad skills when it came to confectionery.

The man in question was hunched over the large sink up to his elbows in soapsuds, Jen chatting excitedly beside him. I went back over to the counter and finished weighing out the ingredients for the extra candy I was going to make. I hadn't talked to Jen, but I was going to be heading back to LA for a couple of days to finalize the divorce. I'd thought about taking the cowards way out and just signing the forms now that my lawyer had given his approval. But there was a part of me that needed to end it face to face. Teddy was a spiteful bastard who'd conned me out of the business, but I'd let him do that by not being present in our marriage. Jen might have gone on about it taking two to make a relationship work, but wasn't I responsible for not paying attention to what had been going on around me?

The thoughts weighed heavy on my mind as I lost myself in the one thing that had always remained true to me—making things that others loved to eat.

By the time I'd finished, both Jen and Lee had disappeared into the store and I could hear voices which meant we'd opened. I glanced around the almost tidy kitchen, a smile spreading over my lips. For all of Lee's clumsiness, he had proved me wrong—the guy worked hard. He never complained and he always had a smile for the customers. Not that I'd watched him, but I'd noticed in passing when I'd gone into the store with a fresh tray to replenish the shelves, even though it wasn't what I normally did. I'd found myself lingering out the front, listening to him explain the complexities of candy making. I guess I should have figured out at that point that he had more than a passing interest. I'd assumed he was just trying to impress the boss.

Did he have aspirations of becoming a confectioner? Or was he just using Sweet Haven as a stepping stone to something else? Would he use my name to gain entry into a cooking school? My smile dimmed. Was he going to be like Teddy and use me? *He's not your boyfriend or your husband. Remember you've sworn off men!*

I might have sworn off men, but I wasn't blind, deaf, dumb, or stupid. Even if Lee was a little on the thin side, he was very pretty. He was also very bubbly and outgoing, the complete opposite to me. The guy would never be interested in a cranky, old chef. *Really, then why does he look at you like you're covered in chocolate and he wants to lick you clean?*

After only four days, I was already noticing how expressive Lee's face was. Years of working in a competitive business and striving to keep on top had left me intolerant of others more often than not. I hated making small talk or trying to be overly nice, so I'd stopped, and the result was a grumpy old fucker. Or so Jen often pointed out. Up to now I hadn't cared, but...

Jen appeared through the kitchen door. "Garrett, do you have any more of those cherry liqueurs? Eileen is after a box for her hubby for his birthday."

"There's a tray at the bottom of the third cooler." I hadn't even finished speaking before she was on her way over there. "Only take half the contents out as I'm planning a road trip for a couple of days. You'll need to make the supplies last until I get back."

The hand reaching for the cooler paused, Jen glancing back at me with her brows arched and her eyes showing concern. "Please tell me you're not going back to LA to see that asshole."

"I wish I could. I need to sign the paperwork and finalize things." I couldn't explain it to her in a way she'd understand, but it was the right thing to do.

"Honestly, big brother, you're opening yourself to more heartache if you go back. He stole your business. He cheated on you. What is there to finalize?"

Glancing over at the door to make sure her strident tone hadn't drawn any attention from Lee, I answered. "I know what he did. But I was partly to blame. You know how single-minded I can be. How would you react if your partner was more interested in his own fame than you? Would you wait about in the hopes of him noticing you?"

A scowl appeared, her hands moving to her hips. "Listen, he has a mouth. At any point, he could have said, 'hey stop being a dickweed and pay me some attention.' He didn't, he used you, and stole your business to sell to his new fuck buddy. That's vindictive and mean. Teddy was always like that. You just never saw it. You were too blinded by the fucking polish he'd coated himself in!"

She was just getting into her stride when Lee appeared in the doorway. "I'm going to shut the door so that the customers can't hear you." He disappeared as fast as he'd appeared in the first place.

Fuckity fuck! Could this get any worse?

Jen shook her head. "Go and do what you need to do, but remember this... that man never loved you. He loved what you could offer him. He didn't work to make your business grow. That was all you. He sat back and let your passion drive you both forward. Let me ask you this. Once the business got off the ground, how much time did he spend helping you?"

Slam dunk! I felt the ball fall through the hoop as Jen took what she needed from the tray and walked back over to the door. She paused, giving me a sad smile. "You shoulder the blame, and that's why I love you. Your grumpiness hides the huge heart hidden inside. Teddy took that heart and stomped on it to get what he wanted. You deserve better, no matter what you think you should've done. You deserve to be loved."

A ball of emotion I wasn't used to feeling lodged in my throat as she disappeared into the store, the door closing softly behind her.

Both my legs and hands shook as I walked to my office and sank down in the chair with everything Jen had just said on replay. Had Teddy ever loved me? The ache developing in my chest suggested that Jen could be right. I'd long since resigned myself to no longer feeling anything for Teddy, but for however many years I'd loved him with all my heart. I'd lain the blame at the door of work, putting distance between us because of my singlemindedness. That it was all on me, and no one else. But if Jen was right, had I been flogging a dead horse from the very beginning?

Did it matter now? Teddy couldn't hurt me any longer. He'd gotten what he wanted—the business, and a new man to dote on him. What had I gotten out of it? Money, and a reluctance to put myself out there to date?

It wasn't as if the town of Sweet Haven was full of available gay men. *What about Lee?* I shot off the chair at the thought. Nope, too young... and... I'd need to think of other excuses seeing as that was the best I could come up with at the moment.

Pushing the turmoil to the back of my mind, I headed back into the kitchen to check I'd done all the tasks written on my list which would free up the next two days. Was it a mistake to head to LA? Possibly. Then why go?

No real answer coming to mind, I shook my head as I checked my list, hoping I wasn't making a big mistake.

7
Leeson

I waited until the rush was over before picking my moment to talk to Jen about what myself and half the store had overheard. Jen was by no means quiet when she got on her high horse about something. If her rant was anything to go by, she evidently disliked Garrett's ex-husband. It had hurt my heart though, at how brutal she'd been at dismissing Teddy's love for Garrett. Was she right? Had the guy been a total dick to Garrett? Or was she just biased?

I guessed it could be both.

Nobody really knew what went on behind closed doors between a couple. I rubbed at my arm, the one Davey had broken in a fit of rage. We'd been together for four years, and I'd only stayed that long because he'd threatened me repeatedly with things he would do to me, my family, and Ollie, if I left him. Fear was a funny thing, clouding all reasonable judgement and leaving little sense behind. It was only once he'd broken my arm that common sense had returned. Ollie had also been having issues with his boyfriend, so we'd taken it as a sign, saying a quick goodbye to our families, grabbing what we needed, and then hightailing it out of town.

For the first few months, it had been hard to always look over my shoulder. But that had faded with time, and now I barely gave Davey a second thought. Unless the weather got so cold that it made my arm ache, but thankfully that wasn't that often.

"You've got a look on your face like you've got fish stuck under your nose. What's up? Is it the conversation you overheard?"

Jen opened the door for me to step in. I did so, avoiding answering with the truth. "Yeah, I heard most of it. It was hard not to." I glanced back at the closed door that led to the kitchen. "Was Teddy really that awful to him?" A wave of warmth heated my cheeks as I glanced at Jen to find speculation in her eyes. "There wasn't much information about their marriage, or the reason for their divorce on the internet," I confessed, hoping she wouldn't judge me for being interested. *Nosey, you mean.*

"No, Teddy wouldn't want to tarnish his polished image," she spat out.

"Oh." I didn't know what else to say. I wasn't sure if confessing that I'd also thought the guy looked a little too polished for my liking would set her off again.

You're just jealous!

I shut out the voice, turning my attention to the counter as a shy-looking girl with bright, golden curls and a fresh face walked up to it. She smiled, revealing a mouth full of braces, and I judged her to be about fifteen.

"What can I tempt you with?" I asked, offering her a big grin. After a couple of hours of folks coming in non-stop to buy their guilty pleasures, the shelves were fairly depleted. Like most mornings, Ollie had been first in line, wanting to see what taster treats Garrett had on offer. I wasn't a candy eater, but I loved to be creative. Ollie, though, had a sweet tooth. When he'd first mentioned a store opening with the same name as the town, I'd thought it was a bit twee. Now, I thought it was the perfect name for a place that sold candy. The store was a haven for those who wanted to treat themselves or their loved ones.

"Do you have any soft candy that just melt in your mouth?" She opened her mouth to point at her braces. "I'm struggling with the hard candy I usually like. They get stuck to the metal, and my Momma has banned me from eating them."

She wore a crestfallen expression that I immediately wanted to rid her of. "I think I might have the answer. Do you have a particular flavor you like?"

After fifteen minutes of going through the trays and giving her a couple of free samples, we found one she loved. Her preference was for soft fruit flavors. I found three she liked that could be sucked and that melted on the tongue. Hopefully, her momma wouldn't be pissed that she'd left with a box of every flavor.

"You've a real talent, you know that." Jen stated as I removed two empty trays and placed them on the counter.

"Thanks. I want people to walk out happy."

"They definitely do that. Did you see how that girl was fluttering her eyelashes at you? She was blushing all over the place from the attention you were giving her."

I glanced over at Jen, my pulse skipping all over the place. "Do you think she thought I was hitting on her?"

Jen's head tilted back as she roared with laughter. It took her a minute or two to get herself back under control before she could answer me. "Nope, I'm sure she's more astute than to think a gay man was hitting on her."

"Oh… erm… okay then." Given that it had only been four days since I'd started working with Jen, I hadn't yet brought up my sexual orientation. I might have been a friendly sort, but I tended to keep that private until I got to know folks better. *It's not like you have a boyfriend or anything worth talking about! Stop reminding me.*

"Is it a problem that I figured it out? The way you look at Garrett sometimes makes it more than obvious."

"Fuck!" I exclaimed far too loudly, slapping a hand over my mouth as I eyed the store, and then breathing a sigh of relief when I found the last customers had gone. When I looked back at Jen, she was grinning, her eyes gleaming.

"Please tell me I'm not that obvious?" When she nodded, I buried my head in my hands.

"I'm not sure Garrett has taken his head out of his ass for long enough to have noticed, so don't stress about it."

Alarm made my stomach jump, twist, and dive like a gymnast as I peeked between my spread fingers. "But *you* noticed. That means he might have too! I swear I didn't apply for this job to hit on your brother. I... you see... the thing is–"

"You have an interest in confectionery and want to learn from my brother."

I sagged as I dropped my hands from my face. "Yes, I do. I couldn't believe my luck when you put out the advert. I've been saving up for the last couple of years. A little here and there so I can go to the culinary school they have a few towns over. I'll never be as good as your brother, but I want to see what I'm capable of with some training."

"I can't judge whether you're as good as my brother, seeing *as you never gave me any chocolate to try*." She emphasized the last part as she walked over to me. "All I'll say is this. If you'd made something that wasn't any good, Garrett would have been more than vocal about it. He just can't help himself. Negative is his first line of defense. I'm sure that's what they taught him in Paris." She shrugged, her eyes crinkling with displeasure.

"You really think he liked my chocolate?" There was a blossoming hope in my chest that I couldn't quell. His lack of reaction earlier had stung. Although, he had moaned. *Was it a moan? Maybe he was choking? Give over, he was not.* Had he hidden the box because he liked the chocolate and didn't want to share? It was a possibility.

Jen nodded enthusiastically. "Yes, I do. I know my big brother. He wouldn't share with me, which tells me everything I need to know. You'll see. He just needs time to think, to figure out what you put in the chocolate before he'll say anything."

She didn't say anything more as she suddenly noticed the time and left in a hurry to get to a hair appointment on time. That left me to tidy up, alone with my thoughts. Apart from my utter clumsiness, the last few days had been amazing with Jen more than willing to show me everything and answer all my questions.

Garrett in the main had remained silent. He worked with such an intense focus that it was a little intimidating to witness. Because he was super organized with his ingredients, it made it easy to follow what he was doing. He seemed oblivious to the chaos he created as he worked, which had come as quite a surprise. If he could use every pot he would. My back and arm muscles had gotten quite a workout, and although I wasn't working a fourteen-hour day, it often felt like I had. Not that I minded, not when being close to Garrett more than made up for it.

The guy was just so... everything. A shiver ran down my spine, my cock taking an interest in where my thoughts were heading. Shutting them down immediately, I went back through to the kitchen to wash the trays. The kitchen was empty and I had to quash my disappointment.

He's your boss! Davey was your boss too and look what happened there.

Telling myself that, did little to stop the questions from filling my head. Where was Garrett? I was sure he hadn't slipped past me to head to his apartment. Had he left town already? Was he that eager to go and see his ex-husband? He wasn't an ex yet, though—the papers hadn't been signed.

A bitter taste filled my mouth forcing me to swallow hard. Filling the sink, I spent the next twenty minutes setting the kitchen and store to rights.

At least you didn't do anything stupid today. That was little consolation though, without Garrett there to witness it. Placing the dirty clothes in the basket allocated for them, I gave the room one final check to make sure I hadn't missed anything before grabbing my bag and leaving quickly through the back door.

It was for the best that I'd not seen Garrett after Jen's outburst. There was no way I could have kept my concern to myself.

I heaved out a sigh as I strode down the sidewalk, praying that the couple of days that Garrett would be away would be enough time for the silly crush I was harboring to disappear.

Yeah, keep thinking that!

8
Garrett

The flight had been short and uneventful. I'd hired a car at the airport to drive straight to my old home. As the gates had opened to let me in, I'd experienced several seconds of doubt about why I'd wanted to do this face to face.

The house was pretty much the same as when I'd left it. The garden was not. The gorgeous, landscaping was gone, and in its place were several ornate statues of nude males sitting on a large expanse of concrete that had once been grass. It stung a little but I shrugged it off, telling myself that it wasn't mine any longer so what did it matter.

As I got out of the sports car, the front door opened to reveal Teddy. He stood on the step clearly dressed for the occasion. For whatever reason, he seemed to want to impress me. He was immaculately dressed from head to toe in Calvin Klein. His hair was styled to perfection, his expression revealing nothing of what he was feeling. It was pretty much the same expression he'd worn for the last four years of our marriage.

When I was within earshot, Teddy spoke. "I see you made good time. I still don't know why you needed to come in person. My lawyer advised that it was more than agreeable for you to sign the papers and return them through a courier. This person-to-person meeting was totally unnecessary."

I was so used to the attack that I didn't bother to respond or argue back. What was the point? This man was no longer my problem. My palms grew slick as the thought registered. Had I only seen him as a problem? Damn it! Why hadn't I paid attention to what was happening around me?

The reason why I'd needed to come back struck me. This had nothing to do with Teddy. It was about me figuring out what I could have done differently. If I wanted to move forward, then I needed to sort my head out. "Why did you marry me?" The words were out before I registered that that was what I'd wanted to ask, the air lodging in my lungs.

"Because you asked."

The air left my body so fast that for a second the world around me wavered. "That was the only reason?" I whispered.

"You were... so forceful, so full of passion. It was hard to say no, when I wasn't either of those things. I had feelings for you from the beginning." He pushed his hands into the pocket of his pants, his gaze fixed on the ground between us. "I'm a selfish person who needs constant attention. You're all about being the best at what you do, no matter what the cost is."

An ache developed in the center of my chest as I listened to him and, for the first time in a long time, I really listened to what he was saying. He truly was selfish. He'd taken from me without wanting to give anything back. He wasn't even ashamed to state the obvious. I'd just hidden it from myself because I hadn't wanted to see any fault in him.

The final barriers shielding my heart fell away and I bled a little at the loss of something I'd never really had—love. This man had never loved me. He'd loved what I could offer him. I'd just been too blinded by my own faults to see it.

Where did that leave me? Single and alone, I guessed.

I'd tucked the papers in the pocket of my lightweight jacket when I'd gotten into the car to come here. Teddy's gaze swept over me and I was no longer sure what it was that I'd once found so attractive about him. I reached into my jacket and pulled out the envelope as I closed the distance that still separated us.

I gave him a cordial smile, keeping my hurt feelings to myself. I held out my hand. "I felt it was important to do this face to face. Whether you realized it or not, I loved you once. I'm sorry that I got lost in showing you that." As he reached for the envelope, I couldn't help but notice the slight tremor to his hand.

Was he upset? Ridiculous, the man had shown he had no heart.

"Here, I've signed them. That's it, you have your wish that we're no longer tied together. I hope you'll find the happiness you couldn't find with me."

He clutched the envelope in his hand, his face remaining a stoic mask as he nodded. Taking that as evidence that our business was concluded, I pivoted on my heel and headed back to the car feeling more than a little relieved that it was over. At least I had closure now. We'd been honest with each other.

Feeling lighter than I had in months, I reached for the car door, only to pause and look back as Teddy called out, "I'm sorry. You deserved better."

I sucked in a shaky breath, my eyes aching as I nodded wordlessly, quickly getting in the car because I didn't want to reveal how much his "sorry" affected me.

I was already headed back to the airport by the time I'd recovered from my shock, any thought of staying in the hotel I'd booked for the night no longer appealing. All I wanted was to return to Sweet Haven and... I left the thought there. The last thing I needed was to be thinking about a certain cute store assistant.

The previous plan to go and visit my old store didn't feel important anymore, so I followed my gut instinct for the first time in years, parking forty minutes later in the underground parking lot at the airport and returning the keys to the rental car. Back in the airport, I changed my return flight from the following day to the afternoon.

Finding a seat in the first-class lounge, I set my overnight bag on the floor next to me, finally taking a deep breath that didn't feel like it was constricted. Phone in hand, I went to type a message to Jen, but paused, staring at the screen for a long moment. Was I ready for a barrage of questions? What if she rang me from the store and Lee overheard the conversation? Yesterday had been bad enough. The guy already had to think I was a total loser. *Why does it matter what he thinks? Out of bounds, remember!*

Tucking the phone back in my jacket, I pulled out the notepad that I used to write things that came to mind. I'd started a page the day before, writing down what I thought was in Lee's homemade chocolate. I'd eaten three of them so far and I was sure I was missing an ingredient. I'd gone through the doubting stage last night, searching the net for any stores like mine within a hundred-mile radius of the town. There'd been nothing even close, which didn't surprise me as I'd done my research before deciding to put my savings into the business.

No, Lee had made those chocolates. And the guy had serious talent. The question was, did I want to help him cultivate it? *Look what happened with Teddy. That was different. Teddy had talent. He just didn't want to work at it.*

Whereas Lee had a true work ethic. I'd had to run to the store yesterday to grab some ingredients I'd run out of. I'd caught up with several people who were friends of my parents, and by the time I'd returned to the store Lee had already left.

Jen had left early, so he'd been left to close the store and clean down the kitchen. The place had been immaculate, everything back where it was supposed to be. Not even Jen had learned where I liked everything to be in the first couple of months we'd worked together. It had caused many a fight when I hadn't been able to find what I needed after she'd put it someplace that made no sense to me. Lee had gotten it after only a few days. He was evidently very observant, that was for sure.

I sucked the end of my pencil between my lips, regretting not packing the remaining chocolates in my bag.

After an hour of jotting down different things that could be used in chocolate, I still hadn't come up with the missing ingredient. I blew out a frustrated breath as my flight was called. I boarded the plane more than a little miffed at my failure to figure out the missing ingredient.

The flight was straightforward as was the drive back to town. The sun was setting, the heat of the day having dissipated enough that I'd left my jacket on so I could drive with the window open. On my return to town, I drove down the main street, my eyes widening as I got to Sweet Haven. The front window was ablaze with light when there should only have been darkness.

Had Jen forgotten to turn off the lights? My stomach clenched as I drove around to the back of the building to park up. There was no sign of Jen's car as I grabbed my bag and got out of the car. I stared up at the building, surprised to see a light on in the spare bedroom.

What was going on?

Overwhelmed by a sudden urge to hurry, I clicked the fob to lock the car as I moved toward the back door. The fact that it was locked helped to settle my pulse rate that had increased on seeing the light on in the apartment. Jen had probably decided to stay the night and had nipped out to grab something. She often came over and ended up in the spare room.

Feeling a little less anxious, I unlocked the door and walked into the kitchen. I froze at the sight of a half-naked Lee, and another man on the floor cleaning up... God knows what. It took more than a few seconds to register the heavenly scents that clearly had nothing to do with me, and everything to do with the two men now scrabbling about in an attempt to stand. It was only then that I recognized the other man—Ollie, one of my regulars.

He was the easiest to read, fear shining from his pale face. Lee looked more resigned than anything, his shoulders hunched once he'd stood. I did my best not to stare at his slim, hairless chest, his skin the color of honey. My fingers curled around the handle of my overnight bag to stop myself from reaching out.

"Do you want to tell me what the hell is going on here?" I growled menacingly.

9
Leeson

Any blood that had previously been in my head decided it didn't need to be there anymore as I stood on shaky legs, a wave of dizziness following. I blinked twice, hoping I was imagining the man in front of me who sounded more than a little angry.

How the fuck did I explain that I'd had a little accident with one of the refrigerators, causing half of its contents to become inedible after they'd gotten covered in some gooey substance.

"We were only trying to help." Ollie offered up while I was still frantically trying to come up with something that wasn't going to get me slung out on my ass.

One glance around the disaster zone of a kitchen had my stomach dropping to my feet, the crushing reality that I wasn't going to be able to fix this leaving me close to tears.

I sniffed, Garrett immediately holding up a hand, his expression pinched. "No, you do not get to cry. Look at my kitchen! Look at it. It's a fucking disaster zone in here. You need a fucking warning label," he roared.

Ollie cringed, hobbling closer to me as if I could protect him from what was coming.

The blue of Garrett's eyes were dark pools reminiscent of a stormy sea, anger rolling off him in waves. "I'm going up to my apartment. I'm going to pour myself a large glass of something to drown out this image. And when I come back, I want my kitchen returned to the way it was before I left this morning." He marched past the both of us, his jaw set.

It was only when I heard the door above us slam that I remembered having stripped off my dirty clothes in his lounge. I'd been too busy ringing Ollie in a panic to ask for his help to have moved them.

I groaned in despair. I was so fucked right now that I doubted I'd be able to sit comfortably for a year once Garrett had finished kicking my ass.

"Do you think he's a hitter?" Ollie whispered fretfully.

I hugged him to my chest, realizing I hadn't gotten fully dressed after taking a shower. I'd been too intent on making enough treats to replace the ones I'd ruined. Could this day get any worse? I eyed my naked, scrawny chest as all the plans I'd had to keep this a secret flew right out of the window. Jen was not going to be happy when she found out she'd wasted all this time on me, that was for sure.

What about the man upstairs?

Focus on the clean-up, come on, focus on that.

The mess on the floor was a pot of sugared candy that had tipped off the side in my haste to get everything done. It had left the tiled floor a sticky mess, as was Ollie and myself.

I eyed Ollie. His plaster cast was covered in who knew what. Whatever it was, I wasn't sure it would come off. "Listen, maybe you should go. I'm positive that if Garrett was going to lash out, he'd have done it when he came in to find this"—I waved my arm around the messy kitchen—"utter chaos."

"I feel bad leaving you. I can help with the dishes. I can lean on the sink to keep the weight off my sugared plaster," he said, eyeing his left leg.

A giggle escaped from me, and then another, and before I knew it both of us were howling with laughter. I wasn't sure whether it was partly hysteria, but I couldn't seem to stop. It was several minutes before I'd gotten myself under control enough to start the mammoth clean-up required.

After an hour and a half of going all out to get the place back into some order, as well as remove the stickiness coating just about everything, we finished the clean-up. I sent Ollie home before checking for one last time that everything was back where it should be. I'd made a note of all the things I'd used so I could replace Garrett's stock. Certain that he would throw out everything I'd made, I braced myself and went to face the music, resigned to meeting the lion in its den. Would he be drunk?

You're about to find out!

Shirtless, and more than a little self-conscious of my nakedness, I climbed the stairs and knocked on his apartment door. The air I sucked in stayed put as I prayed to whoever might be listening that I could keep it together until I got home.

The door opened and I licked my dry lips. Garrett hadn't only gone to get a drink. Hell, no. He must have decided to have a shower too. His chest was as naked as mine, only his was covered in droplets of water clinging to the thick, dark hair and leaving me thirsty for a taste. I had no idea how long I'd stood there gawping like a fool before he coughed, and I realized my gaze hadn't gotten past the towel slung low on his hips revealing naked skin.

"You better come in." Garrett no longer sounded angry. If anything he seemed resigned as he stepped back to gesture at the area close to the sofa. "I think you might want to collect your clothes."

A bubble of hysteria rose up inside me and I struggled to stop it escaping in a fit of giggles as I strode over to the pile of clothes I'd stripped off earlier. I was about to pick them up when Garrett pushed a hand holding a grocery bag in front of my face. "Here. You better use this, or you'll only make more of a mess."

Unsure whether it was humor I could hear in his voice, I glanced sideways, only to regret my decision given that I was still bent over. With my eyes level with the blue towel, all sensible thoughts flew right out of my head as I realized he was naked underneath. I swallowed hard, doing my best to shift my gaze away, but my eyes weren't feeling particularly co-operative. They were going to be getting a serious telling off later. But at the moment all they wanted to do was stare, and imagine what Garrett would look like if the towel accidentally slipped.

"Are you finding something of interest down there?" This time there was no mistaking the humor. I blushed as I went to snatch the bag from him. Only Garrett tutted and moved his hand back. Before I could fathom what he'd planned, two strong hands took hold of my shoulders. And then the world simply disappeared.

His lips were as ripe as any peach. They tasted faintly of alcohol, but there was also a sweetness that melted me from the inside out. Any thought that he'd be rough and hard disappeared as he coaxed me to part my lips. He shifted and I felt like I was floating. It took several seconds to figure out that he'd effortlessly lifted me, the springy, damp hair on his chest rubbing against my naked skin. Sensation flooded my body and took control of my libido, my legs wrapping around his waist to cling on.

The moans that filtered past the lust could have been mine, or they could have been his. I couldn't focus, not with his tongue dipping into my mouth to slide over mine in a caress that made my toes curl in my sneakers. All my attention was focused on how sensitive my mouth was as he sipped at it like it was a fine wine to savor. It was heady and intoxicating to be treated this way. It seemed to go on and on before he stopped, my chest heaving from lack of oxygen.

Sensation after sensation registered along with the arousal I was sporting in my jeans. My cock was throbbing so painfully that I was sure that if I moved I'd come in my pants. "I never meant to do that..." He paused as if he was struggling to find some way of justifying the fact he'd blown my mind from a simple kiss.

There was fuck all simple about that kiss.

I waited to see if he was going to say anything else, my lips tingling as I licked them. Please don't let him regret it, please.

"I want to be sorry, but I can't say I am," he growled, sounding anything but pleased by the confession.

Warmth filled my chest and my lips stretched into a smile. "I'm not sorry," I confessed breathlessly.

"This is not a good idea. I'm not looking for a relationship."

"Who said I was?" I struggled in his arms until he let me slide down his body. His cock pressed against mine and I groaned. The second my feet touched the wooden floor, I stepped back, even though my base instinct was telling me to yank the now tented towel off him and do all the dirty things I'd imagined doing to him, things I denied thinking about late at night to myself. Only now I couldn't deny them, not with a half-naked man in front of me.

I was going to go to hell. I really was.

10
Garrett

What had come over me? Why the hell had I just kissed Lee? If I needed to ask, then I was clearly in need of some serious help. I stepped away from the far too tempting man who was eyeing me with a hunger that stole my breath away. "Can you go and put some clothes on?" Maybe I should do that too!

As if he'd read my mind, Lee's gaze traveled down over my naked chest to the towel that didn't manage to hide how aroused I'd gotten over the kiss we'd shared. His mouth should be outlawed. It tasted like heaven. Give over!

Lee dithered for a second, chewing on his kissable lower lip before pivoting and heading off in the direction of the spare room. I eyed the pile of dirty clothing that remained on the floor. What the hell had happened in the kitchen? After cooling my jets with a large scotch and a shower, I was still struggling to figure out what the heck could have happened to create such a mess. My heart had sunk at the utter disaster that had been my orderly, clean kitchen just that morning.

Shaking my head, I walked to my bedroom to dress in sweats and a T-shirt. By the time I returned to the lounge, the clothes on the floor had disappeared and a bulging paper sack sat by the front door. There were no gloopy stains on the wood flooring, the room looking as it had when I'd left it fourteen hours earlier.

Lee stood by the door fidgeting with the hem of the chef's top he'd opted to wear to cover his chest. The memory of his warm, silky skin pressed against mine made my arousal that had diminished from thinking about the kitchen spark with a renewed life. You can stop that right now.

Lacking any real conviction, I pointed to the door. "Let's see the damage, and then you can explain to me what happened… this time." The man was a walking disaster, he really was.

I'd noted the scar on his right arm. Now I was wondering how he'd not gotten more. He remained silent, wearing a solemn expression as he stepped to the side to let me pass. He followed me, the sound of his sneakers the only noise as we entered the store.

I braced myself at the kitchen door, sucking in a deep breath as I recalled how bad it had been. Holding my breath, I pushed open the door. The air was expelled noisily as I paused mid-step, my eyes widening at the immaculate kitchen.

"That was fast work," I muttered, my heart hammering against my ribs as I walked farther into the room, my gaze sweeping the kitchen and finding nothing out of place. How was it possible that he could create such chaos and then make it all disappear?

Lee gave a slight shrug. "You see, the refrigerator broke and I was worried it would cause an issue to the candy inside it. So, I thought I'd see if I could fix it. Only there was this yucky substance inside the box at the back that somehow managed to get inside, and it ruined several trays of candy. I called Ollie and he came over to help, because I thought if I made some things to replace the stock, you wouldn't be mad at me and fire me. But then my clumsy ass knocked the pot off the counter, and the sugary mix I was working on kind of ended up splattering over every surface. I'm really sorry. I was only trying to help, I swear." His face was flushed, sweat beading on his top lip by the time he'd finished speaking.

My head whirred as it tried to process what he'd said in a grabbled rush. "The refrigerator broke. Why didn't you get Jen to call the repair man?"

His expression turned sheepish as he glanced around the room. "Jen... she... had a few things to do... so I said I'd close up."

"You mean she left early? For what? A nail appointment? Or was it waxing this time?" I refused to let out a sigh, swallowing it down instead. Jen was a princess who loved to preen. I'd forgotten about her habit of skipping out at the end of the day if she could get away with it. I was going to have words with her. If she'd only stayed put... But then you wouldn't have gotten to kiss Lee.

Argh fuck!

I ran my hands through my hair as the scent from earlier registered. Even with all the cleaning Lee had done, the unfamiliar scent still lingered in the air. I sniffed. "What did you make to replace what was damaged?"

Lee hopped from one foot to the other, the color draining from his cheeks as he eyed the end cooler that had been empty before I'd left that morning. The thing now contained several different trays full of candy and glossy-looking chocolates.

"Did you do all that?" I could hear the shock in my own voice. He must have been at it for hours to have created so much. Any doubts I might still have harbored about him not having made the chocolates he'd given me, disappeared.

"Yeah." That one word held a world of challenge, and he stood a little straighter as if daring me to argue.

Instead of debating if he had or hadn't made everything in the glass-fronted cooler, I walked over and opened the door. A delicious scent followed the blast of cool air, my mouth watering. I eyed each tray, trying to decide what to taste first.

"The ones at the top are something I've been trying out. The coca beans are something I get from Brazil. I used up my remaining supply on those. They have a unique flavor that's slightly bitter, but really great at adding depth to the taste of the chocolate."

I glanced back over my shoulder. "Is that what you used in the chocolates you gave me?"

"In part, but I added a Mexican spice I found. Oh boy, it's great at balancing certain flavors, like mint and rosemary. It adds something, right?"

The way he spoke with such enthusiasm and knowledge of what he was doing, made me wonder why he was wasting his life washing dishes and serving customers. I'd need to think about that more, once the delectable man wasn't so temptingly close.

Even though he was still fidgeting with the hem of his top, Lee's eyes glowed with an eagerness that I once remembered staring back at me from my own reflection in the mirror. His passion and excitement were as intoxicating as the kiss had been. I tightened my fingers on the cooler door in the hope it would stop me from grabbing the man who was eyeing me with a nervous excitement he couldn't hide.

"Are you going to try one of the others?" he asked hesitantly, his brow furrowing.

"Which one would you recommend? Which is your favorite?" My heart beat a little faster as he came closer, the scent of sugar and something more masculine surrounding me.

"I don't have a real favorite as such. But the almond crunch with the buttercream would be one of my top picks if I were to choose." He kept his gaze fixed rigidly on the cooler as he reached past me, lifting a chocolate to hand it to me. "This one."

His fingertips were cool against my skin as I took the chocolate he offered. Our gazes connected, the room disappearing as something hot and potent passed between us. I felt the power of the moment deep inside me. It was more than lust, more than a desire to take him right where he stood. There was something intangible I couldn't name in the pit of my stomach that lurched as if I was a rodeo cowboy.

The chocolate became slippery in my fingers from the heat of my body, giving me an excuse to break the connection. My heart thudded painfully in my chest as I lifted the chocolate and placed it in my mouth. I closed my eyes, blocking out Lee's intense stare as I focused on the candy melting in my mouth. The balance of flavors was perfect, as was the silky-smooth chocolate coating my tastebuds. Before I could think better of it, I licked my sticky, chocolate-coated fingertips and groaned in delight.

There was a sharp exhale, my eyelids drifting open to find Lee's bright green gaze fixed on my mouth. His lips were parted, his chest heaving, the desire that had sparked between us in my apartment flaring to life again. I was totally screwed.

Lee stepped forward, looping his arms around my neck. Unused to a man taking the lead, it threw me for a moment, but I went with it as Lee tugged my head down. "This is a bad idea."

"The worst," he mouthed against my lips.

All common sense disappeared as his mouth claimed mine in a heated kiss that scorched through me faster than a summer bush fire. It left no part of me untouched, even though it was only his mouth and hands touching me. I followed where he led, his tongue sliding over the seam of my lips until I opened for him. And then the sweet taste that was uniquely him was all there was.

This wasn't the soft exploration of the first kiss we'd exchanged. This was all about hunger, his mouth clinging to mine and causing utter havoc without any thought to how we'd cope when we stopped.

Feeling more than a little out of control at him taking charge, I felt compelled to do more than be passive. My hands roamed down his sides until I reached his hips. Then I cupped his pert ass and lifted him. He moaned, his tongue getting frisky in a way that made my toes curl. Holy fuck, the guy could kiss!

The handle of the cooler door digging into my back gave me an unwelcome reminder of where we were. I staggered a little as Lee's hips rolled, his arousal pressing against mine, and his magic mouth working to steal what few brain cells I had left.

I grunted as Lee pressed more firmly against me and I collapsed back against the door. "Fuck, we need to move," I growled against his hot, greedy mouth.

But Lee refused to give up on his assault. "Why?" he mumbled, sounding as breathless as I was before returning to kissing his way along my jaw. His teeth raked over the stubbled skin, leaving a trail of sensation that left me struggling to remember why we needed to move.

A blast of cool air at my back gave me enough of a reality check to manage to step away from the cooler and toward the kitchen counter. Lee wasn't playing fair though, his fingers creeping up into my hair to tug hard enough that I felt the bite of pain all the way through my body before it lodged in my cock. I had a thing for hair pulling and, boy, was he yanking my chain right then. My legs shook as I attempted to focus on where we were in relation to the counter. After three attempts I managed to reach the counter, parking Lee's ass on the stainless steel.

Panting as much as if I'd run the Boston marathon, I tried to make my hands and cock see sense as Lee worked to destroy all semblance of control. Never in all my years with Teddy had I lost control enough to rut like an animal in the kitchen. I'd have been mortified if anyone had told me they'd lost control in a working kitchen. Yet here I was contemplating taking Lee on my shiny kitchen counter.

As that thought finally registered, I grabbed hold of what little defense I still had against the stunningly sexy man who was sitting staring at me like…

The thought remained unfinished. I held my hands up to ward him off. "We're in a working kitchen," I said in a strangled voice. I took several inhales, hoping that would get rid of the cloud of need to ravish Lee right where he was, looking all kissable and dishevelled.

I took a step back, trying not to notice the disappointed expression Lee was now sporting along with his solid erection.

"I'm sorry," he muttered, his eyelids dipping to conceal his thoughts.

"Don't! I'm not sorry. I just"

"You're not?"

A hopefulness I was defenseless against had me closing the distance between us to cup his warm cheeks. His lips were puffy, and his chin and cheeks were covered in stubble rash. He'd never looked more beautiful to me and that scared the shit out of me.

I'd told him I wasn't looking for a relationship, and by God I'd meant it. I'd not gotten out of one relationship only to jump straight into another. You split from Teddy months ago. How is that jumping straight into another relationship?

I couldn't find a valid answer to that, not with Lee looking all sexy and kissable, and his eyes begging for more. I laid my forehead against his. "I signed divorce papers today. I need time to digest that." It wasn't the complete truth. I needed time to think about Lee and figure out what I wanted, but he didn't need to know that at the moment.

The ache in my groin suggested that I go with the flow and see where this would go, but that wasn't my style. I'd only had two previous sexual partners and one of those had been my partner for twenty years. As much as I wanted this to just be about sex, that wasn't how I was built. I gave Lee's soft lips a gentle kiss, stepping back as he moaned. "I think you need to go home. You have an early start tomorrow and it's already been quite the eventful day."

Ten minutes later, I shut the door and locked it behind Lee. I leant my head against the cool wood, my lips still tingling from the kiss I hadn't been able to resist giving Lee before he'd left.

"How am I supposed to keep my hands off him when all it takes is one of his hopeful expressions to turn me into a gooey mess?" I muttered to the empty kitchen.

With no easy answer coming to mind, I dragged myself back to the kitchen. I ignored the cooler with the tempting candy inside. They were very much like the man who'd made them—far too addictive if I wasn't careful.

11

Leeson

Garrett wasn't playing fair. He really wasn't. He hadn't even mentioned what had happened in the kitchen three days earlier. He'd kept stoically silent. Whatever he'd told Jen about the broken refrigerator, she'd not brought it up, and I hadn't known what to say about it.

Tomorrow was my first day off since I'd started at the store, Jen so desperate to show me as much as possible with her departure date growing ever closer. The excitement I usually felt at having some downtime to play in my kitchen at home, though, was missing. How could I be excited when Garrett had been as silent about the kiss as he'd been about the things I'd made for the store?

Oh, don't get me wrong, the cooler was now empty, the candy and chocolates all sold. Garrett had told Jen to separate them from his with a sign to say they were something new to the store. Had he done that so he couldn't be blamed if people hated them? I huffed out a breath, the question remaining unanswered just as it had for the last few days. Why don't you just ask him why he sold them separately?

Sweat gathered beneath my chef's top and I blamed it on the hot water I was elbow deep in.

"You're quiet this morning. Is something wrong?" Jen asked in a low whisper.

Smiling at her, I shook my head. "Nope, I'm just thinking about what I'm going to do with myself tomorrow." I'd used up all of my coca beans on the disaster, and I was still waiting for my new supply to arrive. So it wasn't like I could make a start on the ideas I'd had for a new chocolate while thinking about Garrett's peachy lips.

A stirring of desire unfurled in the pit of my stomach and I concentrated on the grimy pot in front of me willing it away.

"Do you want to come and work with me in the kitchen?"

Garrett's question made the pot I held slip out of my hands and into the water, the water splashing both me and Jen. I gave her an apologetic smile, or at least I hoped that was what it was. Given the buzzing going on in my head, I wasn't too sure what I was doing.

Jen laughed as she turned toward her brother. "Say what? Did you just offer Lee the chance to work with you?" She dropped the cloth she'd been using to dry the pans, poking fingers in her ears and wiggling then around. "I think I need to visit the doc because I'm sure I just heard you speak."

"Fuck off," he growled, sounding even more menacing than usual, color flooding his cheeks as he didn't bother to look in my direction.

I was worried there going to be another argument. The pair of them were prone to them, having no problem expressing themselves nosily if they needed to. "Yeah, I'd lov... like that." I hoped Jen hadn't noticed my slip-up.

When she continued to stare at Garrett with an expression I couldn't interpret, I released the breath I'd been holding and picked up a cloth to mop up the water.

As I stood, my head connected with the lip of the sink in a demonstration of my usual clumsiness. "Ya shitty bastard!" I cried out, my vision filling with blinding white spots as the room spun.

"Now what?" Garrett shouted. The hands that took hold of my arms were gentle though, as he guided me to his office and pushed me down into a chair. To my surprise, he crouched down and started to examine my head. His fingers ran over my scalp, my groan escaping before I could think better of it.

Jen appeared behind him with an ice pack in her hand. I kept my gaze fixed rigidly on her as Garrett continued to run his fingers through my hair. I started to breathe heavier, my body not getting the message that he was only concerned that I might have hurt myself, not trying to cop a feel.

"You're looking a little flushed there, Lee. Maybe this ice pack will cool you down," Jen stated, her voice quivering with suppressed laughter, and her eyes sparkling.

"I'm fine." I sat back, hoping Garrett would get the message as I continued to avoid looking at the man who knelt at my feet.

"I heard the thud from the other side of the kitchen. Don't tell me you're fine when you were moaning just a second ago," he accused in a grumpy, no-nonsense tone.

Warmth blossomed, spreading up my chest and heading to my face. The acute embarrassment didn't abate as I finally met his stare, trying to convey without words the reason I'd moaned.

It took a moment, but eventually the light dawned in his eyes, his nostrils flaring. He didn't take his gaze off me as he said, "Jen, give us a few minutes."

I didn't look at Jen to see her reaction. I wasn't sure I could look away anyway, not with Garrett finally giving me his full attention. The door closing was the only sound for several seconds as I waited for Garrett to say something, something that would rid me of the horrible ball of tension I'd had in my stomach ever since I'd come in the day after the kiss only to be met with silence.

"Does your head hurt?"

That wasn't what I'd wanted to hear, but at least it was something, and it was accompanied by a concerned expression. "It throbs a little."

"Whereabouts?"

I frowned, pointing to the left side of my head just above my hairline. My hand fell uselessly to my lap as he leant forward and planted a gentle kiss on the sore spot.

A soft sigh escaped from my parted lips.

"Is that better?"

Feeling a little giddy, I shook my head to see what he'd do. His lips twitched as he came a little closer. This time he parted the hair, blowing on the super-sensitive spot before pressing his warm lips to it. His lips lingered for what felt like an age, the breath sticking in my chest and my insides turning to jelly.

As he shifted back to stare at me, his expression was the softest I'd ever seen it. A grumpy expression was normally his go-to, and even though, it was usually because he was sick of me, I still found it hot. This look, though. This did things to me that had little to do with desire and everything to do with my heart. My heart fluttered wildly, reminding me of what it felt like when it was more than just simple attraction. I wanted to be able to chastise myself for the new feelings, but with him looking at me the way he was, I was totally screwed. There was no defense that was going to be able to protect me from that look.

I traced a fingertip over the side of his face, following the lines around his eyes as he continued to wait for my answer. Only I couldn't even remember my own name, never mind the question he'd asked me only moments before.

"Do you need another kiss?"

"Fuck, yeah." There wasn't time to prepare myself as he captured my mouth in a heated kiss that was again different from the others we'd shared, his mouth seeming to devour mine. I felt owned in a way that should have made me run for the hills. Only that was the last thing I wanted to do, so I wrapped my arms around his neck and clung on instead.

He overpowered my senses, his flavor all I could taste. I was achingly hard and needy for more, my chest heaving as he finally pulled back.

"You make me lose my ability to think rationally."

From the way his lips were pursed, I wasn't sure whether that was good or bad. "I'm going to take that as a compliment."

"Why doesn't that surprise me," he replied as he stood.

Level with his groin, I could see just how much the kiss had affected him. For the first time in a long time, it felt good to be me. It was a heady feeling to know I had the power to make this man lose himself in me.

"Stop smirking at me like that." Garrett scowled, tugging at his chef's top in a way that had to be an attempt to cover up his obvious arousal.

My smirk stayed in place as I stood, placing my hand in the center of his chest and trailing it down to the waistband of his pants. I stopped just shy of the cock pressing against the fabric. His eyes narrowed on me, but he didn't move. "I think you like me smirking at you. So why would I be silly enough not to give you what you want?"

"If you don't move that hand, I'll be giving you more than you bargained for. It'll be a show my sister might never recover from!"

I chuckled at the visual that popped into my head but removed my hand anyway, not wanting his sister to be witness to anything. "Is the offer about tomorrow still on the table?" I held my breath as I changed the subject, far too anxious for his answer to be able to breathe.

"Yes. I've been thinking about all that wasted talent. Washing dishes and serving customers might be a good job, but it's not what you want to do with your life, is it?"

I shook my head. What was the point in denying it? I wanted to be in the kitchen creating magic, not washing dishes. Was he going to make my dream come true?

"I want to see how you handle yourself when you're not making candy due to some disaster, even if your disaster candy and chocolates did fly off the shelves."

"Really, they liked them?" I all but danced on the spot, Garrett's mouth morphing into a wide grin for the first time. The excitement at what he was potentially offering faded in comparison to Garrett's smile.

Holy fuck, it was killer!

I stood transfixed, unable to look away.

He rubbed at his face as if he was searching for something. "Have I got something on my face? You're staring at me funny." The smile disappeared, the scowl I was used to seeing reappearing.

"You were smiling. It's the first time you've done that since I've met you."

"Don't be ridiculous."

"Whatever, man." I squeezed past him, opened the door and skipped back into the kitchen, my mind already on the things I wanted Garrett to teach me. Tomorrow morning couldn't come soon enough.

I barely held in the complaint, the excitement that had kept me floating for the last twenty-four hours dissipating faster than a balloon losing its air. Garrett was in full teaching mode, talking about stuff I already knew from my reading over the last nine years when I'd been intent on replicating everything I'd learnt from the internet.

"Are you listening to me?"

I nodded, gritting my teeth to keep from complaining as I reminded myself for the umpteenth time that he was being helpful in taking his time to show me the basics. Basics I already knew, but whatever.

Another hour passed and I was beyond bored, Garrett explaining every step to making a plain, sugared candy that I could have made in my sleep. I stifled a yawn, working hard to keep an interested expression in place.

Living with Davey had taught me how to pretend interest if I wanted to avoid a punch to the face. There wasn't much else to thank the asshole for, but he'd taught me patience.

"Are you paying attention?" Garrett's voice interrupted my thoughts and I nodded. "Then talk me through the six steps I've just gone through."

I resisted rolling my eyes as I went through each step without so much as stopping to think. He looked pleased, giving me a small smile and patting me on the arm like I was a child who'd just answered a homework question. It was irksome and I had to bite my lower lip to stay quiet.

"That's wonderful! Now let me explain about the tempering of chocolate, and then maybe we can give you a simple recipe to follow and see how you do."

I figured he wasn't trying to be patronizing, but the way he was talking to me was starting to make my blood boil. He'd tasted what I'd made. Did he think it had been a fluke? Was that why he hadn't bothered to establish what I was capable of? Or to ask what I understood about the basics when it came to confectionery? The guy was treating me like I was... simple! "Can I ask a question?"

His brows rose at the terseness in my voice, his head tilting to one side with an odd expression on his face before he nodded.

"Have you ever taught before?"

This seemed to throw him as he rubbed at his temples. "I've done teaching demonstrations, so yes."

"But, have you ever taught an individual?"

"I just—"

I held up my hand to stop him. "No, you said you gave demonstrations. It's not the same."

His eyes hardened, his jaw becoming fixed in position as he gritted out, "What is your point?"

There was anger sparking in his eyes, but I didn't back down even though the fear that I'd felt in the past when I'd seen a temper like his would have had me retreating. There was a part of me that understood that no matter how mad Garrett got, he wouldn't use his fists to express that anger, so I stood my ground. "You're wasting my time and yours with all these basic instructions. I love that you want to show me each step, but I'm bored witless. Sorry if that sounds selfish, but I've been playing around in my kitchen and learning things for the last nine years. If you'd asked me to explain all these steps before we started, I could have still explained them and shown you what I already know."

His jaw thrust forward, his hands balling at his sides. "Then why the fuck am I wasting my breath? Why didn't you mention this when we started?"

The accusation hit its mark and I gave him a sheepish smile, feeling more than a little guilty. "I found it cute in the beginning. But then you started to go into way too much detail and it got boring."

"Are you saying I'm boring?" He took a menacing step toward me, his eyes back to the stormy blue that made my blood heat and desire swirl in the pit of my stomach.

I remained still, even as my insides jumped with giddy excitement from provoking the beast. He took hold of me, hauling me against his hard body, the air leaving my lungs. Ohhhh!

If I'd known I'd get this reaction, I would have spoken up sooner.

The back door opened and Jen appeared. Her mouth fell open as her gaze fixed on the two of us, Garrett not seeming to have noticed that we had company.

That was confirmed as he gave me a little shake, growling, "I'll show you boring."

His mouth claimed mine and I closed my eyes, not caring about our spectator as he stole my breath away with the heat of passion he unleashed on me. His hungry growls fueled my desire and I wrapped my arms and legs around him, holding on for all I was worth.

My body ground against his, the aching throb I was becoming used to whenever he touched me leaving me helpless to stop my hips from rolling against his.

"Fuck, I want to eat you alive," he moaned into my mouth, sounding as desperate as I felt.

"Could you wait to do the eating part until after I've left? I enjoy a good show as much as the next person, but it's only fun when it's not my brother."

Jen's sarcastic comment made Garrett jerk back as if he'd been slapped. His cheeks were flushed and his lips slick from mine. I wanted to ask him to take me upstairs more than anything, but I sensed his withdrawal even before he scowled at me as he carefully lowered me to the ground. He said nothing as he walked off toward the restroom, shutting the door with more force than was probably necessary.

"Wow! When he offered to train you, that was not what I thought he meant." Jen wore her glee like a badge of honor as she blew on the backs of her fingers and then rubbed them on her T-shirt as if she were congratulating herself for something.

My eyes narrowed on her. "Did you employ me in the hope of setting me up with your brother?"

She shrugged, but there was a glimmer of satisfaction in her eyes that she couldn't hide.

"You totally set us up, didn't you?" I tried to muster some outrage, only it was literally too hard to do, given the throbbing of my groin which hadn't disappeared even though Garrett was no longer trying to kiss the living daylights out of me.

She made a zipping motion with her lips before taking off her jacket and hanging it on the hook by the back door. "Don't mind me. I'm just going to wash up these pots and then I'll be out of your way in no time at all, so you can carry on with your... training." She waved

111

her manicured fingers in the air as she skipped over to the full sink, humming, 'Here comes the bride' under her breath.

"You know that's not funny."

"Really?" She giggled, not looking in the least bit bothered by my comment.

I gave up, returning the cheeky grin she was aiming at me. "You're a bad influence. You better hope that when he comes out of the restroom he's in a better mood."

Her gaze travelled past me to the hallway where the restroom was located. "Please! I really don't want to think about what he might be doing in there to put him in a better mood." She shuddered and gave a dramatic sigh before looking back at me. "I'll just hope for his usual grumpy self."

Secretly, I hoped for that too.

12

Garrett

Wednesday was my day off. It was the day where I caught up on things I'd let slide during the week. Only today, all I could think about was Lee downstairs playing in the kitchen without me.

After returning from the restroom last week, I'd gotten him to talk me through everything he'd learned on his own. Which had turned out to be a fucking lot. The guy was like a sponge. One big squeeze and he'd talked my ear off for hours about different processes, coca beans, sourcing ingredients, and anything else that happened to strike him. I'd been more than overwhelmed by just how much he knew, and it had left me in little doubt that he should be working as a trainee confectionery chef.

In the end, I'd encouraged him to be as creative as he wanted, which had given us some much-needed distance while my sister pretended not to be watching us. The smile on her face had given me pause that this had somehow been her plan all along. Get her brother and the cute, single guy together. How did I feel about that? I was too old to play games, even if my sister wasn't, but I couldn't find fault with who she'd picked. Lee was... special.

Sweat beaded my brow and I struggled to breathe past the tight band holding my chest hostage. The week I'd spent thinking about that mind-blowing first kiss had left me in no doubt to what I wanted. I normally struggled to muster passion for anything but my work, but with Lee, it was definitely there. He challenged me in so many ways, and this past week had surpassed himself in creating stunning pieces of chocolate. The chocolate creation he'd made the day before, rivaled anything of mine from the past. It had stood three-feet-tall, in the shape of a giant, grinning toad, the lily pad it sat on designed to look just like the real thing.

There'd been no more words exchanged about training him. Although there were probably things I could teach him, I wasn't sure what they were at the moment. What I did know, was I'd be a fool not to offer him a trainee position in my kitchen. Someone who could do what he could, shouldn't be wasting their talent. I'd mentioned it to him, asking him to give it some thought.

Why had he never had any official training? I'd listened to him talk when Jen had been in twenty questions mode. There'd been no mention of any higher education past his high school diploma.

I chewed on my thumb, a habit I'd mostly grown out of, as I stared out the window at the busy street below. The queue to come into the store had grown again today. Was that because of Lee's candy?

I'd been stopped no less than a dozen times in the grocery store over the past week to talk about the new candy. I'd purposefully asked Jen to place them separately, for no other reason than to gauge people's reactions.

Where did all this leave me? With a possible new partner?

Anxiety clutched at my stomach, swirling beneath the excitement as I tried to analyze whether it was my dick or my head putting that question front and center. Both was the obvious answer. Closure with Teddy had freed me somehow, and whatever gloominess had hung over me since my return home, had gone. I wasn't sure whether it was signing the papers to finalize things, or whether it was Lee himself. All I knew was that he made me feel... young. He makes you feel a damn sight more than that!

A wry chuckle passed my lips as I watched folks leave with bulging bags of sweet treats. Was I jumping in too fast? Was I on the rebound from Teddy? It was a possibility. I'd already suffered disappointment by jumping in too fast and not paying more attention to what was happening in my own life.

I'd promised myself I wouldn't do that again. Where did that leave me? I wanted Lee to train with me full-time. Should I keep it just business? An ache developed somewhere deep in the center of my chest at the idea of not exploring what was growing between us. Lee hadn't hidden how he felt. There'd been some hesitation which I didn't fully understand. Maybe it was because I was his boss and he needed this job. I wasn't stupid enough to think he couldn't, or wouldn't, find a way to fulfil his passion at some point in the future.

I tugged my thumb from my mouth. Shaking my head, I shoved my hand in my pocket before I could do any more damage to the nail. There was a brief knock at the door, then the sound of a key, Jen appearing a few seconds later. I gave her a smile as I turned to face her. "What's up? Has Lee created some other disaster that I need to fix?"

Jen tipped her head back as she roared with laughter. After filling her in on what I'd found on the night of my return, I'd given her a stern talking to. Not that she listened to me.

"Nope, he's been on his best behavior. I wanted to talk about what your plans are now that we've discovered he can make sweet delights. I know you spoke to him a couple of days ago." Although she sounded happy, her brows were drawn together.

"Sit." I indicated the bar stools at the kitchen counter. "Do you want a drink or something?"

"I had one not long ago." She perched on the edge of the green leather stool, one of her legs swinging back and forth.

Taking the seat next to her, I leant an elbow on the counter, resting my chin on my palm as I eyed her. "What do you think I should do about Lee?"

Her eyes sparkled with mischief. "If it was me, I'd tie him to my bed and do all manner of things to him until he confessed the recipe for the salted butter chocolate twists, but that's just me."

I spluttered and coughed, slapping at her hand. "Hey, no talking about tying anyone up." I shuddered, trying to block out the image of my sister touching... my man.

"What? You asked." She snatched her hand back and giggled. "Okay. Let's be serious. I think you've

116

already made up your mind, and if I'm honest so has Lee. That means we need to find someone else to train to take over my job." There was resignation in her tone as she gave me a half-hearted smile.

"You're right, and I'm sorry as this could delay your plans." I patted her arm. "Was there anyone else you interviewed that was a good fit?"

She sucked her lower lip between her teeth. "There was a girl, Nese. I could ring her and see if she's still interested."

"Okay, give her a ring and let's see what we can sort out. I'll need to speak to Lee to see if he's as keen as you think on being my—"

"Sex slave?"

"Would you stop that. It's gross. You shouldn't be thinking about me and sex!"

"I'm only messing with you. Come on, where's your sense of humor? Anyway, I'm sure that whatever you have in mind, Lee will be more than interested. He's had sad puppy dog eyes all week because you've not paid him any attention."

He'd had a lot of my attention, but it was a relief that neither Jen or Lee had noticed that. "It's my workplace, not some pick-up joint."

"Can I just point out, that it was you lifting Lee off the floor and kissing the living daylights out of him last week."

Despite doing my best to hide my embarrassment at being called out for unprofessional behavior, warmth spread to my face. Never in all my years of working in a professional kitchen had I ever lost control like that. "I thought we weren't going to be talking about my sex life?" I pointed out, hoping it would stop Jen dead in her tracks.

Only the little minx didn't stop. "Hey, as I said, I wasn't the one kissing the heck out of someone right in the middle of the kitchen."

I held my hands up in defeat as I stood. "Point accepted. Can we get back on track? Can you ring this Nese person? Then I'll talk to Lee about what happens next. And whatever thought just crept into your filthy mind, keep it there."

She blew me a kiss, not looking at all chastised given the light in her eyes. "You're no fun. I'll go and search out the forms I filed in the office and ring her now." She paused on her way to the door, turning to give me a serious look. "Be careful with Lee. He might like your grumpy ass, but he's been hurt badly in the past. If you genuinely have feelings for him, then don't mess him about. He's a great guy."

She disappeared out of the door, leaving me wondering what Lee had shared with her about his past. Heading back to the bedroom, I changed into a pair of running shorts and a T-shirt. A few minutes later I was running down the street toward the large park in the middle of town which had a large lake at its center and a track used by joggers and walkers all year round. The town of Sweet Haven was never truly cold. The weather was mild in the winter and blistering hot in the summer. To my mind, spring and autumn were the best times of year, where it was warm enough to be outside without needing a jacket.

Spring was just around the corner. I could feel it as I picked up my pace, ignoring the slight chill in the air. I nodded at several people as I kept up my pace, starting to feel the endorphins kick in and my mind become clearer.

I wanted Lee to work with me. Was I willing to take a risk and ask for more? When I'd taken the same risk with Teddy, it had been twenty years ago when I was young and felt like the world was my oyster, and it had seemed less important. Would the age difference between us make this a non-starter? What about the chemistry between us? Was it just chemistry, or was it something more? And if so, was that enough? I thought you weren't going to kid yourself. There's more than that between you, so stop denying it. The question was, whether I should ignore it and focus on the business? Like that worked well for you last time.

I growled, increasing my pace in the hope it would stop me from thinking so hard.

Life's too short not to take a risk. Oh, shut up!

Several laps later, with my head not much clearer than when I'd started out, I jogged home. I was a sweaty, dripping mess, my legs tired and aching. No one paid me any mind as I stepped into the packed store. Lee was busy at the counter, smiling at a young girl as he explained the choice to her. His expression was so eager and full of joy that it melted the last remnants of my resistance. My lips tingled with the need to go over to him and kiss that delectable mouth. That wasn't going to happen, though, not when the store was full. I reluctantly walked past the queue, heading over to the door which led to the apartment. As I sidestepped a customer, Lee glanced around, giving me the sweetest smile. How was I supposed to resist him?

The seconds stretched as I stood there dripping with sweat. Lee's head tilted, one brow arching. What was wrong with me? Why was I letting this man get to me so much?

Because he's everything you never knew you wanted.

I heaved a sigh and walked through the doorway before I gave folks something to really gossip about.

13
Leeson

As Garrett disappeared through the door in shorts that should be outlawed for public use, I wet my lips, trying to recall what the girl had asked. When she pointed to the third tray down, I reached for it, thankfully recalling that she wanted a dozen of the strawberry-dipped, sugar-coated candy in the shape of hearts for her boyfriend.

Valentine's Day was only a week away, and as yet I'd not worked up enough courage to ask whether I could make some special Valentine's chocolates to sell. Given Garrett's offer to make me his trainee chef, I'd had little chance to think about much else, never mind to ask him if I could do something extra. Garrett didn't usually go for large scale chocolate creations in the store and I wasn't sure why. There was plenty of counter space for some. In the previous store he'd owned in LA, he'd sold all manner of things. I'd checked it out online. I couldn't figure out why he hadn't bothered here. Was I being too pushy?

I rolled my eyes to the ceiling, forgetting that I was supposed to be boxing candy. Jen fired a questioning look in my direction and I gave her a bright smile, refocusing on what I was supposed to be doing.

When there was a lull an hour later, my thoughts returned to the best way to approach Garrett. Ever since Garrett had worked with me to assess my level of competence, I hadn't thought about anything other than the things I'd be able to make now that I had access to his high-quality equipment. You've thought about more than candy! My cock twitched, rubbing against my underwear and reminding me of exactly what I'd been thinking about.

A wave of heat spread over my body, images of Garrett's wet, naked torso filling my head, along with the memory of the kisses we'd shared. Why hadn't he tried to kiss me again? I nibbled on my lower lip as I organized the trays with the remaining candy and transferred them over to the other trays. The sound of Jen returning from the kitchen grabbed my attention. She'd been a little weird since returning from speaking to Garrett this morning. Wednesday was the only day he didn't work, and I had to say that I missed his presence in the kitchen.

Jen rested her hip against the counter as she stared at me. "If you keep nibbling on your lip like that, you'll make it bleed. You got something on your mind, Lee?"

"I... have some ideas about Valentine's, and I was wondering if I should talk to your brother about them. He's been real tolerant of me being in his kitchen, and I don't want to overstep, ya know?"

"Tolerant! He's shouted at you no less than ten times in the past week. Is that your idea of tolerant?" She laughed, her cheeks pinking and her eyes gleaming with repressed humor.

"That might be the case, but it's only because I'm so clumsy. I stepped on his foot, whacked his elbow with the big pot, and hit him on the shin with the tray." I stopped as she held up a hand, tears running down her face.

"Alright, I give up. He had good reason to shout. You're a walking disaster," she choked out past her laughter.

I groaned in despair. She wasn't wrong. Did that mean Garrett would be turned off by my lack of spatial awareness?

"Stop frowning, you're adorable. And my brother thinks so too. He's just grumpy and forgets to smile. But I've got a feeling you'll change that." She tapped her lower lip, her expression turning serious. "I wasn't going to say anything, but I never was any good at holding my water. Garrett has asked me to ring one of the other folks I interviewed to see if they're still interested in the job."

"Wait. What? Is he going to fire me?" I cried out, the fear all too real.

"Shut up! Why would he do that? He's offered you a trainee position. That's a full-time role. You can't do what you're doing and replace me." She smirked, my stomach turning to jelly along with my knees.

"Seriously?" I felt like I was going to pass out as the room seemed to spin around me. My chest didn't feel right, and it was only when I exhaled that I realized I'd been holding my breath. Sucking in a few greedy breaths, I leant against the counter next to Jen. "Oh, my God! I never realized he meant for me to just work with him in the kitchen?"

A wide grin spread over her face as she nodded. I studied her closely to see if she was winding me up. When all I saw was excitement, I returned her smile, convinced my face might crack given how wide my grin was. "Well, fuck me."

"Pardon me," came an all too familiar voice from behind me.

"Why me!" I muttered under my breath as I turned to face Garrett who was looking as gorgeous as ever, his skin glowing with health and his hair damp from the shower. His T-shirt hugged his barrel chest, making me want to bury my face against it.

"Stop getting all growly. We were messing about," Jen said, jumping to my defense.

I gave her a grateful smile before focusing my attention back on her brother, who'd continued to glower at the pair of us. Or at least I thought it was both of us. Knowing my luck, though, it was aimed just at me.

Garrett pointed at me. "This is a place of business, not some..."

When he appeared at a loss for words, I waited a beat before adding, "a seedy motel for nefarious types?" in an attempt to be helpful.

Jen snorted, Garrett's lips twitching before his shoulders started to shake. "You... there are... no words," he spluttered out before starting to laugh in earnest.

Jen slapped my shoulder as she whispered, "see he's a big softie really," before swinging around and disappearing into the kitchen.

By the time Garrett had pulled himself together, several more customers had come in. I watched Garrett out of the corner of my eye as I served them. Once the store was empty Garrett walked over to the door, my heartrate picking up as he flipped the lock.

His trip back to the counter seemed to take forever as I tried to gauge what was on his mind. Was he going to bring up the subject of my change of job now?

By the time he reached me, I was struggling not to hyperventilate at the thought of my dream coming true, at the prospect of being offered a position in a professional kitchen with a top-class confectionery chef.

"Jen blabbed, didn't she?" He sounded resigned rather than pissed, so I nodded. "I thought so. I wanted to have a serious conversation about what it is that you want."

My eyebrows shot up and I bit my lip to stop myself from blurting out "you," because I was sure that wasn't what he was talking about. It wasn't, was it? "What do you mean by 'what I want?'" There. I'd asked outright and hadn't been struck by lightning. Yet!

He ran his fingers through his hair, something I noticed he did when he was frustrated. That wasn't a good sign.

"You want me to lay it all out?" he asked.

His hesitation was more than obvious. I released a shaky breath and took a leap of faith, hoping like fuck that he'd catch me. "Yes." I gestured around the store before pointing at myself. "I want to know what it is you're offering in relation to the store... and me?"

He ran his hands through his damp hair again, the strands ruffling as he stared intently at me. "I would like to offer you a position as a full-time trainee chef working alongside me. Jen is already looking for someone to replace her... you." His eyes darted to the kitchen door Jen had disappeared through, his brows arching. "But then you already knew that."

When his gaze returned to me, I answered, "Yep."

"About the other thing... I... it's hard for me to..." He seemed unable to finish, taking two deep breaths before shaking his head.

Thinking he wasn't going to say anything else, my heart sank. Didn't he want me? My lower lip trembled, my eyes starting to ache.

"If you so much as release one tear, I swear I'll... I'll spank your ass," he muttered, his face turning a shade of red that wasn't very becoming.

A bubble of laughter gurgled up and got stuck in my throat. I did my best to swallow it back, but he looked so grumpy that I couldn't stop myself from giggling at his discomfort. "You totally didn't mean to say that, did you?" I said, having way too much fun as it distracted me from feeling that he wasn't going to want anything more than a professional relationship.

His gaze became menacing as he stomped around the counter without looking away. "You think I'm joking? That I won't pull your pants down and spank you?"

The blood my brain needed to be able to think relocated itself south at a speed that left me a little dizzy and a hell of a lot aroused. There was no way I wanted him to spank my ass. Did I? I'd never been into any form of violence. Hell, I abhorred it. Davey had made sure of that. Then why was my cock jerking and leaking in my pants at the idea of this man warming my ass?

Lacking the time to give it any more thought, I skipped toward the kitchen door as Garrett went to take hold of my arm. "Come here." His voice dipped sexily, his gaze searing my body as it roamed over me, stopping where my arousal was tenting my baggy pants.

Fuck, I was in so much trouble!

My feet suddenly became cemented to the floor as he smirked, a devilish gleam appearing in his eyes. "You like that idea, don't you?" he whispered against my ear, his hot breath causing tiny shivers to race down my spine.

How the hell was I supposed to answer that without sounding weird and kinky? I was saved from having to by Jen as she called through the kitchen door, "Garrett, the guy is here to service all the appliances. Where do you want him to start?"

I sagged in relief, Garrett giving me a knowing smirk. Desire unfurled in the pit of my stomach as he gave me the sexiest fucking smile. "This isn't over."

I wiped my sweaty brow as he walked off into the kitchen. "I hope not!" I muttered under my breath.

The rest of my shift went by in a flash as I tried to avoid spending too much time in the kitchen. I grabbed my backpack and was getting ready to leave when I smelt Garrett's sweet fragrance seconds before his chest pressed against my back.

"Where do you think you're going?" he mouthed quietly in my ear.

A shiver ran through me as his tongue touched the sensitive skin on my ear. "I've finished," I squeaked.

"I think you might have missed some things... things that still need to be cleaned."

The words were said in a sexy way, but I was confused by what he meant. I twisted my neck to look up at him. His face was so close that I could feel the warmth of his breath over my flushed skin. "What needs cleaning?"

"My lips."

It was the only warning he gave before swooping down to claim my mouth. Any thought of protesting was lost beneath the wave of pure lust caused by his tongue probing between my parted lips. The kiss left me in no position to argue, and fighting the urge to climb him. I groaned when I couldn't do as I wanted. Given our awkward half-twisted position, my neck had started to ache.

"Jeez, what is it with you two? Why am I always catching you both locking lips?" Jen said, laughing.

Garrett was the first to let go. If I'd expected him to be embarrassed, I would have been disappointed. He looked... smug.

He winked, strolling off wearing a smile that left me weak at the knees and in need of a heart doctor.

I grappled with the door handle, fleeing into the street, my chest feeling like it was going to burst with the realization that this man had the power to hurt me like Davey never could. He'd done it with his fists. Garret wouldn't need to do that. All he'd need to do was walk away and find someone else to love.

14

Garrett

Leeson had been evasive all morning. He hadn't made his usual effort to talk to me as he did every other morning, regardless of whether I answered or not. He'd kept to himself, burying himself in being creative, the number of trays of decorated chocolate hearts filling every counter as they increased.

"Are you hoping the folks of Sweet Haven are going to give their loved ones a chocolate heart for Valentine's Day?" I joked.

His grunt was so unexpected that I glanced over at Jen, who seemed to be wearing a matching expression to mine—one of concern. Was he worried about my threat to spank him? He had left in a hurry yesterday after I'd kissed him. Was that why?

I ran my hands through my hair, completely forgetting that I'd been rolling out a sticky mixture to cut into candy shapes. Jen started to laugh as I attempted to tug my sticky fingers from the strands of hair they were stuck to. "Fuck's sake!"

Leeson's laughter joined Jen's as he glanced in my direction for the first time in three hours. "I thought I was the only klutz in this kitchen."

"Ha ha ha," I muttered, stalking off to the restroom to wash out the crap stuck in my hair.

"Need a hand?" Leeson called as I got to the door.

The temptation to say "yes" was there, but then I caught Jen sniggering with the new girl, Nese. When Jen had contacted Nese, she'd discovered the girl was still looking for a job. Nese had jumped at the chance to start straightaway. She seemed nice enough, and hadn't appeared phased by the state of the kitchen this morning when she'd arrived. There'd been a raised eyebrow when Jen had carried out the introductions, but other than that Nese had followed Jen's instructions and stayed quiet. At the moment, she looked far too interested in what was happening between Leeson and myself. I called back, "Next time you offer, make sure to do it without an audience."

"Funny, big brother, funny." I heard as I shut the door and chuckled to myself.

The rest of the morning passed without incident, Leeson remaining far too quiet for my liking. I'd grown to enjoy his constant commentary about anything and everything that floated through his head.

With Jen and Nese busy in the store, I walked over to Leeson as he started to clear down the worktops. Unlike me, he preferred to clean as he worked. "Is there something on your mind? You've been really quiet this morning."

The hand holding the cloth trembled as he whipped around to look at me. He stared up at me for a long time, emotions flittering across his face too fast for me to be able to interpret what was going through his head.

"Are you just messing with me?"

I jerked. "What? I'm not sure what you mean. Messing with you?" My brow furrowed as I tried to make sense of what he'd said.

"Are you leading me on? You said you weren't looking for a relationship the week before last. Then you start talking about spanking me, and I can't seem to stop thinking about that. Is that weird?" He didn't let me answer as he barreled on. "Sometimes you act like you wanna be my boyfriend, you know, kissing me in front of people. What is it you want from me?"

Sensing vulnerability, I didn't hesitate to answer honestly. "The spanking thing was spur of the moment, but I could certainly get behind it if you were interested?" I swallowed in an attempt to moisten my mouth. "If I'm honest, when I said I didn't want a relationship, I was scared of what that might mean for me. I meant it when I said I don't do casual. I never have. I've had two sexual partners in my life."

The flush of warmth trying to crawl its way up my neck made it obvious that I was finding this conversation embarrassing, but I'd never been in the habit of lying, not even to myself. Well not intentionally anyway. "When I said I needed time to think about us"—I pointed at him and then at me for extra emphasis, Lee's eyebrows arching—"I meant it. My ex did a real number on me. He conned me out of my business so that he could sell it to his lover. He used my temper against me to take what I'd worked so hard to build. It left a sour taste in my mouth that makes me scared to try without thinking about what happens next. I've had time to think about it now, and I'd like to ask if you want to go out with me?"

His sympathy changed to a stunned expression. "Like on a date?" he squealed, bouncing on the spot.

I laughed at him. "Yes, like a date."

"What about the work stuff?"

"What about it?" I frowned, trying to figure out what was bothering him. Did he not want to date me while we worked together?

"You mentioned a new contract to train me, and you haven't sorted that out yet, and now you're talking about dating. Don't get me wrong. Fuck, I want both, I do. But what if..." his gaze dropped to the counter.

My stomach clenched in response to what he was saying. He was right. I'd jumped from one thing straight into something else. The thing was that he did that to me, and for the first time in my life I was acting in a way I'd never done in the past. Was it wrong? I wasn't sure, but I was prepared to go along with it. He didn't realize how big a thing this was for me. I offered him a smile, hoping it would help to alleviate some of his fear, as well as bolstering my own confidence. "Let's take this one step at a time. Think of it like a new recipe. You have to start with figuring out what ingredients work together by trying out different things. I want to try different things with you to see if we can create a new recipe together." It sounded so corny that I cringed, but it was too late to take it back.

His face glowed as he dropped the cloth and stepped closer to me. "You mean it? You really want to try dating and working together? I swear I'll never be mean like your ex. I'm just not that kind of person." He scratched his head, his face clouding with concern. "My past experience of a relationship where you mix work and dating has been a bit of a disaster. Much like yours. But without the cheating and stealing a business part."

The forlorn expression that graced his face set off warning bells in my head. My gaze narrowed on his left arm as he took hold of it, rubbing at the scar on his forearm. My pulse spiked and I got an uneasy feeling in the pit of my stomach. "How did you get that scar?" My question came out as no more than a whisper.

My fear cut off the air supply to my chest, my throat constricting as I waited for him to answer while staring into eyes that held a wealth of pain.

"My ex, who was also my boss... his answer to my clumsy behavior was to try and beat it out of me. It's a long and sordid story and I won't bore you with the details. Let's just say he decided that breaking my arm would show me who was boss." His eyes filled with tears that he was struggling to blink back.

In two strides, I had my arms wrapped around him, hugging him into my body. "Shush, it's okay." They were stupid words. It clearly wasn't okay. But given the seething anger which accompanied the knowledge he'd been abused, I couldn't think straight.

"I'm fine. I'm not so much upset about Davey. That's in the past. I'm just worried about what this means to us. I... I want this to work so bad, but whenever I get involved with someone it all goes to hell and I don't want that to happen between us," he finished on a sob.

His tears made me feel like utter crap and I struggled not to be grumpy at him. I bit my lip instead, remaining silent as I held him in my arms, occasionally running my hand up and down his back. He made little snivelling noises that were quite cute, but his sobs tore at my heart.

Minutes passed before he finally pulled back, his face blotchy and his eyes swollen. There was a rosy flush on his damp cheeks. "Thank you," he said, hiccupping before walking off toward the restroom.

The cloak of dignity he wore made it difficult not to go after him and... and what? Emotions I wasn't sure I was anywhere near ready for made their presence felt, an ache developing in the center of my chest. Too fast, way too fast. Why was it too fast? Who the fuck knew?

When Lee returned five minutes later, I was no closer to figuring out a way of making him forget his shitty ex. The only option I could come up with was to take him for a jog. It always helped clear my head. "Do you want to go for a jog?"

His brows pinched together. "Jog? As in walking at speed?"

It took a concerted effort not to laugh at how alarmed he sounded about it. "Yes, it's a form of exercise that can help clear the head and make you feel good." I offered him a reassuring smile, only to be met with an expression that looked anything but convinced.

"Erm, I... you see, exercise and me... we aren't friends and never have been."

"Don't be ridiculous. Everyone is friends with exercise."

"Not me, I can assure you," he muttered so quietly that I struggled to hear him.

"Listen, why don't you give it a try with me? I'm sure you'll enjoy it." I walked over to Leeson and took hold of his hand to tug on it. "Come on, I'll take it easy on you."

With a little more convincing and a lot of cajoling, Leeson changed into a pair of shorts and a T-shirt that he'd left in my spare room.

Thirty minutes later, I had hold of his hand as we walked down the main street in the direction of the park. Several people nodded, some not quick enough to hide their obvious interest in our joined hands. Leeson didn't seem to notice. Or if he did, he didn't say anything. He was too busy chewing on his lower lip, his gaze fixed somewhere on the ground in front of us.

I squeezed Leeson's fingers. "This is going to be fun."

"If you say so."

There was such a lack of conviction that I increased my pace, wanting to show him how wrong he was. By the time we reached the park he was already panting, and I had a moment of panic that I might have made a mistake. Everyone enjoys a bit of exercise. Lee will be no exception.

"We need to do some light stretches so that you don't pull any muscles. Then we'll do a couple of laps around the lake."

Leeson's lips parted. He was eyeing me like I'd suggested he remove a hot tray from the oven without a protective glove. When he said nothing, I released his hand to lay a gentle kiss on his parted lips. "I'll give you a reward if you do two laps with me. How does that sound?"

He groaned, but looked resigned to his fate as he nodded. "It better be a good reward," he grumped, sounding far too much like me.

"It will be, I promise." I kissed him until the taste of his mouth was all I could think about. When I lifted my head, his mouth gave chase which didn't hurt my self-esteem in the slightest. "Let's do it."

It only took half a lap to realize that I'd made a huge mistake. Lee was about as coordinated as a newborn baby giraffe. His legs seemed to go in different directions, while his arms had some sort of odd rhythm that made him look like he was flailing half the time. He'd managed to kick me twice and knock into me four times. Sweat was dripping down his face and he looked just about ready to keel over.

15
Leeson

What had possessed me to think I could do this? In what universe had I ever been any good at sport? None! Garrett had a lot to answer for, for fluttering those baby blues at me and enticing me into madness. The reward better be fucking epic after doing this.

I whimpered, swiping at the sweat which was trying to burn my eyes right out of my sockets. My vision blurred and I blinked, losing my balance and, for the umpteenth time, managing to kick out at Garrett's ankle. This time he staggered, and before I had time to release a relieved breath that he was okay, he lost his footing. His arms flailed in slow motion and as he was so close to the water's edge, he had nowhere to go, but in. I reached out, but it was already too late. There was an almighty shout as water cascaded all over me.

My already blurry vision got even worse, and I lost sight of Garrett, chilly water dripping down my face and over my sweat-soaked T-shirt. I tried to swallow but my mouth had dried faster than the time I'd accidently used salt in a recipe instead of sugar. Garrett surfaced from the water, spluttering and cursing up a storm with his face a dripping mask of fury.

Oops!

I squeezed my lips together at the urge to laugh as he swiped hair out of his eyes. My shoulders shook as I took a step back, and then another, my legs shaky. He dragged himself up the bank until he stood in front of me. Was that steam coming out of his ears? He eyed me with something akin to disbelief. "How the fuck can you turn a simple jog into—"

"You know I'm a klutz," I butted in, not sure I wanted to hear whatever else he'd been going to say. I pointed at my own dripping clothes. "I'm wet too."

He growled, approaching me with a look in his eyes that I'd seen before—desire. I took a few steps backwards, not paying any attention to what was behind me. It was only when the back of my leg hit a bench that I stopped. I glanced around looking for an escape, giving Garrett enough time to grab hold of me.

I squealed as he lifted me up, his hands under my armpits as I dangled in mid-air. "What am I going to do with you?" he growled low in his throat.

Any hope of being able to control the desire flooding through me, died, as his lips laid claim to mine and he mouthed, "That spanking you were so interested in... is going to happen the second I get you back to the apartment."

As if I wasn't already in enough trouble, my mouth forgot to let my brain engage before speaking, "Promises, promises. I thought I was getting a reward, not a punishment."

He eased back a little, the devilish glint in his stormy blue eyes leaving me breathless and anxious to get back to his apartment. "Oh, don't you worry. You'll be getting a reward." He lowered me to the ground, his gaze dropping to my shorts. His chuckle was nothing short of sinister as he grinned. "Let's go. You can jog all the way back."

He didn't give me a chance to argue as he took hold of my hand, tugging me along with him as he started to jog. I squealed as my cock rubbed maddeningly against the confines of my underwear, the wet clothes chafing my skin as I tried to keep up with Garrett.

It seemed he was a man on a mission, the pace not slowing. Although, I was too busy trying to catch my breath to care. Oxygen deprivation meant I had to settle for cussing him in my head rather than aloud.

Didn't Garrett know that people could die without oxygen? Was he trying to torture me because he'd fallen in the water? It was a possibility, but then I reminded myself that he'd already been torturing me even before that.

The second the store came into view I groaned in delight. Garrett didn't even appear winded when he eventually slowed to a stop outside it. His face glowed with a sheen of sweat. Even though his hair was still dripping wet, and his clothes weren't in much better shape than mine were, he still looked amazing. Whereas I was sure that I resembled something dragged out of the bottom of a dumpster. It was so unfair.

"Right troublemaker, inside."

That grumpy voice was going to be the death of me. I was sure of it. I meekly followed Garrett, ignoring the laughter from behind the counter as Jen caught sight of us both.

Garrett didn't say anything as he walked through the store and straight up to his apartment. Any hope I might have had that he'd had time to rethink the spanking were dashed as he shut the door behind him and turned to face me, saying, "Strip. I want to see those ass cheeks when I make them glow."

It was the fact he didn't even try to hide his desire that got my trembling hands moving. He leant back against the door, watching my every move as I stripped off the soaking clothes. Once they lay in a pile at my feet, it took all of my effort not to hunch over as his gaze roamed hungrily over my body.

My own cock plumped as his hand dropped to the front of his shorts and he stroked his cock before pointing to the sofa. "Get down on your knees in front of the sofa with your chest on the cushion."

The rasp of his voice seemed to caress my eager cock, and it bobbed in total agreement to his suggestion. This was totally insane. Yeah, but you're gonna do it, aren't you? Holy fuck, I was! Ever since he'd first mentioned it with that "intense, sexy as sin, I want to devour you' look," I'd wanted it. If that made me weird, then who the fuck cared. It was between me and Garrett. It was no one else's business.

My ass cheeks clenched as I walked on unsteady legs over to the sofa.

"God, your ass! It's so fucking perfect," he ground out, his voice sounding pained to my ears.

I stopped questioning what was about to happen as I got down on my knees. The silence that followed was torturous as I waited.

There was a sensation of heat behind me, just before his hand slowly caressed the back of my thigh and up to the curve of my ass cheek, where it lingered. Warmth spread through me and I pushed back into the gentle caress. It had been over two years since I'd been touched so intimately apart from my own hand, so this... this felt huge.

"Have you ever been spanked?" I lifted my head to shake it before laying it back on the cushion, unable to loosen my tongue from the roof of my mouth. "Then, this is a first for both of us."

I croaked out, "You've never done this with anyone?" Not that it made any difference. Now that we'd started down this path, I didn't want to get off.

"No, I've never been tempted. But you, you make me want all manner of things I've never wanted before." His lips touched the swell of my buttock, followed by the tip of his tongue. "I've thought about what it would feel like to heat your ass. To see the red glow and know that when you sit down, you'll think of me. Fuck, is that too weird?"

I chuckled, raising my head to look back over my shoulder at the man knelt behind me worshipping my ass. "Maybe, but it's a choice we're making together." I stressed the last part as I held his gaze. "I've been hit with violence, but never with passion. That's what you want, right?" There was a degree of uncertainty in my voice.

"I'll never hit out in violence. That's not who I am." He lowered his head to lick my left cheek, his gaze revealing his need. "This is different. But know this... if you don't want to do this, just say so."

The pregnant pause that followed showed how serious he was. My heart thudded hard against my ribs, something important passing between us. That depth of feeling kept me kneeling, my cock throbbing with just how much I wanted him. I wanted him with every fiber of my being, and not just because of who he was, but for the man he was. "Do it."

The killer smile was back and, for the first time, I was glad he only aimed it at me, and not at anyone else. It was mine and mine alone. The intensity of my need to be claimed by this man left me sucking in a deep breath as I laid my flushed cheek against the soft cushion and lifted my ass in silent invitation.

Garrett pressed a kiss to my ass, his weight shifting until I felt the press of his erection in his damp shorts press against my hip. The air stirring above my ass was my only warning as a stinging pain lit up my ass.

It took a few seconds for the warmth to follow, heat spreading to my aching balls. The second spank came a few seconds later, as if Garrett was giving me the opportunity to say no. Only I didn't want that. I wanted… more.

The sound of his hand slapping my ass was drowned out by moans and groans—his and mine. I humped against the sofa, not caring that I was smearing pre-cum over the cushion. The ache in my sac was like a pot of sugar coming to the boil. If Garrett wasn't careful, I'd erupt all over his sofa.

I shifted to reach under me, needing to do something to alleviate the tension.

"No, Lee. No touching your cock.

I groaned, pushing back into the next spank. "Oh fuck, it's not enough. Harder!" I cried out, finding it hard to believe I was asking him to spank me with more force. The light swats had me hanging on the edge, but although they stung, they weren't enough to give me what I needed.

Was I going to regret this later? Possibly. But all I wanted to do was come, and if he wasn't going to let me touch myself, he needed to do something to get me there, and fucking fast.

"Are you sure? Your ass is already a beautiful shade of red?" he questioned, sounding a little sceptical as his fingers trailed over my hot skin.

"Please. Either that or touch my cock. I need to come, like fucking now. This is torment, man." I jerked forward as the next hard smack landed on my ass. A burning heat flared in my channel, spreading to my sac and then down to my cock. It burned so good that I mewled and cried, "again," while rocking forward to try and get some friction on my cock.

Several hard spanks later, I was still suspended on the edge of the cliff, tears clouding my vision as I snivelled, desperate and needy. I wasn't sure whether my ass could take any more. I was about to ask Garrett to stop when the tip of his tongue tickled the crease of my ass. "Ohhhh, fuck!"

"You want my tongue?"

Was he joking? I wanted whatever he would give me. "Yes, jeez! That, and whatever else you want."

He chuckled, his warm breath ghosting over my hot ass. Then he got down to business. Firm fingers pried open my ass cheeks and I moaned anew as he nibbled his way down the crease to my clenching hole. His tongue circled my rim, teasing the nerves to life and laving the puckered flesh. He made several grunting noises that sounded downright dirty, my cock bucking as the noise vibrated through my channel.

"You're killing me, please do something."

"I thought I was doing something," he murmured against my hot flesh. Then as if to prove his point, he pressed the tip of his tongue past the tight rim of muscle, the little jabbing motion sending sparks of lust to my cock and my brain short-circuiting. "Ya fucker!" I cried out in a strangled whisper as my cock jerked and cum pulsed from the tip. My eyes clenched shut as I lost myself to the overload of sensation.

On and on Garrett worked to milk me of my orgasm, his tongue continuing to stretch my hole as he pushed deeper. It was as if he was hungry for more of my taste, his own groans heating up my skin.

I was a panting, sweaty mess as I collapsed against the cushion, Garrett finally releasing my ass and shouting, "Arghhhh," before shuddering against my side.

The damp patch on my hip grew as his cock throbbed against me and he released his load. A sense of satisfaction that I'd done that to him caused my lips to lift into a smile. Who knew spanking could be so much fun? I couldn't wait to do it again. Garrett moved back, the cool air hitting my burning ass. I groaned, my cock giving a little twitch.

I lifted my head to look at Garrett, finding him staring back at me with heavy-lidded eyes filled with something I didn't want to examine too closely. "I think

I've found something your clumsiness can't get in the way of." The killer smile was back, my cock giving another twitch, this one even stronger.

To show him that he might have counted his chickens a little too soon, I rolled over to reveal the cum-stained sofa. He lowered his gaze to the stained cushions, releasing a put-upon sigh that did little to diminish the happy glow he wore. "Okay! All that means is that I'll need to keep on trying."

Fist punching the air in my mind because I was too knackered to be able to do more than that, I grinned at Garrett. "I'm game, if you are."

16

Garrett

Could you die of blue balls?

Get over yourself. It's not been that long.

I ran my hands through my recently styled hair, trying to recall why I'd ever thought that sitting Leeson down to have a 'no sex rule' conversation after the spanking until we got to know each other a little better was a good idea. You don't think having your tongue in his ass was getting to know him better?

My hair took the brunt of my frustration as I tried to think about anything other than Leeson's delectable ass.

After Jen's prompting to hire Nese, I'd finally sat down with Leeson to talk through what his new contract would entail. I'd made sure to include a clause that meant he got a percentage of the profits from the candy he made. Today had been Valentine's Day, proving that it was only fair, as it had only taken four hours for the shelves to clear of all the chocolate treats he'd designed and made. They'd literally flown off the shelves. If I'd thought the two-foot chocolate hearts that you could write your loved one's name in had been overkill, Leeson had proved me wrong. Nese and Jen had had to rope in Leeson to keep up with the demand to decorate the darn things.

I walked over to the counter, to where the chocolate treat I'd made last night after everyone had left, lay. I eyed the little cartoon figure I'd made of Leeson critically. Once upon a time I'd enjoyed the frivolous side of chocolate-making, creating funny little characters for my friends. Why had I stopped? They took time and effort for no profit, that's why. I shut out the voice trying to rain on my happy parade. It wasn't welcome.

With it being Valentine's Day, I'd wanted to do something for Leeson, suggesting that we go out for dinner at a place two towns over. The restaurant had been recommended by one of Jen's friends, Cissy, who worked there as a waitress. It was going to be a trek, but if the food was as good as Cissy had said, then it would be worth it.

Would it be too dorky to give Leeson the chocolate in the restaurant? I sighed, placing it back in the box and tying the pale pink ribbon around it before leaving it on the counter. I checked the time, walking over to the window to look out into the street.

Since the jogging incident, I'd not mentioned doing anything sporty to Leeson. Not that I hadn't enjoyed what had happened afterwards. Fuck, I'd come harder than I had in years just from Leeson's pleasure. The man was more addictive than anything I'd ever encountered before. A secret thrill ran through me at the fact that he appeared to feel the same. Over the last week we'd spent a lot of time together. Once we'd finished in the kitchen, we'd taken to going for walks in the afternoon so that I could show him my favorite parts of the town.

He'd finished hours ago. So, where was he? He should have been here by now.

Leeson always tended to be early for everything. He'd explained he did it in case some disaster befell him. Given that knowledge, him being two minutes late made me start to fret. I searched the street again, but there was still no sign of him. I turned and went to grab my phone. Had he messaged to say he was running late? The blank screen said he hadn't. I pressed the icon, the phone lighting up. Where was he? Had he had an accident? "Jeez, stop it. You're acting like an ole mother hen," I muttered to the empty room.

That didn't stop me from worrying though, as I opened my messages. We'd taken to sending silly texts to each other, along with pictures of weird confectionery art. Leeson loved the idea of one day creating something that would be photographed and classed as confectionery art. He loved the fact that several of my sweet creations had been photographed. I'd learnt just how long he'd followed my career. It was both flattering and embarrassing to find out how much he knew about me.

I'd resolved to find out as much about him as he knew about me, but for all his openness he'd been reluctant to share some parts of his past with me. I blamed Davey for that. It had been hard to listen to some of the horror stories he'd told me about how controlling Davey had been.

A loud knocking sound had me dropping the phone on the counter and rushing across the room. A little out of breath, I yanked the door open, only to find my sister stood on the other side of it. "What do you want?" I

149

grumbled, looking over her shoulder to see if Leeson might be behind her.

"That's a warm welcome. It's so overwhelming that I'm at a loss for words."

"Oh, fuck off. What do you want? And have you seen Leeson? He's running late and he's never late. Do you think he might have hurt himself and can't get to his phone?" I babbled, concern taking charge of my mouth.

"You are too cute right now. If I didn't already know how much you wanted his sexy ass, I'd be able to guess." She gave me a broad grin and pointed to the stairs behind her. "Lee's downstairs waiting for you." Her smile seemed to grow even bigger, if that was even possible, her eyes lighting up with a knowledge that left my stomach feeling all kinds of anxious.

"What's going on?"

She laughed, taking hold of my shirt sleeve and tugging on it. "You won't find out by standing up here flapping your lips together."

I flipped her the bird as I strode past her, the chocolate box and my jacket forgotten in my haste to find out what Leeson was up to. As I entered the store, I forgot to take a breath as my eyes filled with tears. He remembered!

Sat on a table in the middle of the store was one of the designs I'd created for a special event in Paris for my graduation. It was The Eiffel Tower. I'd created it as my final piece and it had given me my first taste of success. It had a special place in my heart, as did the man stood behind the table with a nervous smile.

If I hadn't fully understood before just how talented Leeson was, this showed his true potential and talent. It had taken me years to learn the required skills to ensure that the chocolate design remained standing and looked amazing. He'd managed to replicate my piece, the delicate chocolate glimmering with the spun-sugar work he'd added that allowed the light to reflect, making it shimmer and appear as if it were lit up.

I swallowed hard past a lump in my throat. My heart beat erratically as I circled the table. In all the years Teddy and I had been together, he'd never truly gotten how much I loved what I did. Leeson did. It was there in the detail, in every swirl and intricate piece of the design. My vision blurred as I met his stare. "You did this for me? It must have taken you hours! Days even."

He blushed and shrugged his shoulders, the action drawing my gaze to the smart shirt he wore. "Happy Valentine's. I'm glad you like it. And yeah, it was hard to work on it, what with you being all nosy about what I was doing with my time off." He chuckled and gave me an impish smile that made my heart flip in my chest.

"Just, fucking wow! You truly have a gift, Lee. I might never say this again so listen up. You know I'm not good with this shit. I think you've got more talent than I ever had when I started out. If you can create this without any formal training… well, fuck me sideways." I didn't get any further as he flew around the table. He reached out to wrap his arms around my waist, his eyes gleaming as I caught him.

I hugged him into my body, inhaling his familiar, sweet scent as he sobbed out, "You have no clue what that means to me."

If he was anything like me, and I suspected he was more like me than he'd ever want to admit, then I knew how much he needed the validation. I held him tighter, Jen disappearing into the kitchen and shutting the door to leave us alone. I'd thank her later, but all I wanted to do at the moment was kiss this man for understanding me better than anyone else.

I placed my fingers under his chin and tilted his head back. "How did I get lucky enough to find you?" I whispered before claiming his mouth. He moaned, clinging to me as I kissed him with all the emotion rolling around inside me. I struggled to remember the fact that we were supposed to be going out for dinner and that I'd promised myself that we wouldn't get carried away again until we'd gotten to know each other better. How is that working out for you?

I growled as I pulled back, his dazed eyes making me dip my head for one more taste. His lips parted and I was lost to him. I craved his sweetness, his passion, and his desire. "We need to stop if we're going out for dinner," I murmured against his lips, hoping he'd help me to see sense.

"Why do we need to go out when we could just eat each other?"

A groan rumbled through my chest as I put enough space between us to be able to think past the desire to do more than kiss his delectable mouth. "You're supposed to be the voice of reason."

"Who said that? They need to take a hike... the voice of reason is overrated." As if to make a point, he ground his lower body against my thigh, his erection digging into the muscle and leaving me in no doubt about what he wanted.

"We agreed no sex until we get to know each other a little better." I was sweating. I could feel it trickle down my back as he worked to undermine the thin shred of control I still had.

"What do you want to know that I haven't already shared?" He rolled his hips, his eyelids drooping as he started to make a delightful noise.

"Stop it, you're being bad."

"Does that mean you'll spank me again?"

He sounded way too happy about the idea, my cock jerking painfully against the fly of my pants. In a strangled voice, I said, "You're killin' me. I want to make this a special evening."

Leeson heaved out a sigh as he released me. He took a step back, looking none too happy about it, his eyes narrowing as he readjusted his erection. "Okay, I'll let you have your way. But when we get back here, I'm going to expect a reward."

I chuckled. "I think I can live with that."

His brows rose. "Yeah? We'll see about that," he fired back mischievously.

What had I done?

17
Leeson

The drive to the restaurant had taken well over an hour, but Garrett had kept me entertained with stories of his training in Paris. Although they were humorous, it must have been hard to work to the standards required in order to achieve highly in such a competitive field. Was that why he'd developed an outer shell of grumpiness? Probably. There must have been immense pressure on him to succeed and pay his parents back.

Garrett parked up and I stared at the chic-looking restaurant as I got out of the car. The place was everything I'd thought it would be: posh, and not somewhere I could afford in my wildest dreams. You can now, with your pay rise and a percentage of the profits.

Giddy from the knowledge that for the first time in a long time I had the ability to splurge, my stomach did a little rock and roll. The pot of dollars I'd saved burned a hole in my pocket with thoughts of the kitchen appliances I could buy.

I was still floored from Garrett telling me how talented I was, but at least he was now willing to train me in the more in-depth stuff that he could do with his eyes shut. Did he really believe I was more talented than he'd been at the same stage?

A man wearing a smart suit and tie appeared in the foyer of the restaurant, his warm smile pulling me from my thoughts.

"I've a reservation under the name of Garrett Weston. A table for two." Garrett took my hand as the man indicated that we should follow him.

The muted voices and scent of rich food surrounding us left me feeling more than a little out of my depth. The tables weren't all full yet, but those that were occupied contained folk that had made an effort to get dressed up. I eyed my dark pants and the pale pink shirt I'd worn without a tie because I didn't own one. Was I underdressed?

Garrett wore a suit in charcoal grey that fitted like it had been made to measure. Underneath it was a crisp, white shirt and a pale grey tie. I sighed. Even if I'd had anything better to wear, it was too late to change. Was I embarrassing Garrett?

His fingers squeezed mine as if he could sense my unease. "Whatever has got you looking like your puppy just died?"

As we continued to follow the man through the restaurant, I whispered, "Am I underdressed?"

He stopped, making me trip over my own feet, our chuckles following. "You look gorgeous. You know how difficult it was for me to keep my hands off you. Does that answer your question about how you look right now?"

The seriousness of his expression was at odds to the hint of humor in his voice. "Yes. Yes, it does." I squeezed his hand a little tighter.

The head waiter stopped at an empty table that looked like it sat right in the middle of an oasis. Displays of flowers had been used to block others from being able to overlook the table, my heart doing a little skippy thing. Had Garrett asked for this specially?

Did it matter? Not really. Not once the man in question had picked up the rose from the place setting and handed it to me. "For you. I have a little something I made back at the apartment which I meant to give to you, but after your surprise it felt a little too dorky."

Intrigued by the embarrassed look that crossed his face, I sat in the chair the waiter had pulled out for me. My fingers trembled as I stuck the flower under my nose to smell its rich perfume. "Beautiful," I whispered, meeting his gaze as the head waiter offered Garrett the same courtesy and pulled out his seat for him. Garrett gave me one of his smiles that melted me into a puddle as he sat.

I only half-listened as the waiter explained the set menu for the evening with its five different courses accompanied by five different wines. I didn't have the heart to say that I wasn't a big fan of wine as the guy went into detail about the qualities of each wine, and how it would complement the food.

By the time he left I was struggling to keep still in my seat. "Do you think they'll be offended if I don't drink all the wine?" I murmured, checking to make sure the guy wasn't still in earshot.

"Of course he will. He's a wine snob." Garrett said, laughing, the rich sound doing silly things to my belly.

"It's not funny," I hissed back.

He reached across the table, taking hold of the hand that wasn't holding the rose, which I'd not put down yet. "Listen, this was supposed to be a relaxing evening where we get to spend some time together. If you don't want the wine, then leave it. I'll only be having a couple of sips of each as I'll be driving us home."

"Oh, I could drive. You can have all the wine," I offered, giving him a smile of encouragement.

"You drive?"

There was scepticism in his tone. I couldn't blame him, given that he'd witnessed my epic clumsiness up close and personal. "Yes, I drive. I just can't afford a car right now. I was saving all my money to go to the culinary school three towns over."

His hand tightened around mine. "I seriously think that you'll be wasting your money. You have mad skills in the kitchen. What is it you think you need to learn?"

That opened the gateway to conversation, and as the dessert was placed in front of me three hours later, I wasn't sure what had happened to the time. It felt like I'd hardly taken a breath as I'd talked about all the things I'd written down that I wanted to learn. Garrett hadn't once ridiculed me. In fact, he'd listened intently and added some suggestions as I'd enthused about some of the things I'd found on YouTube. "You know you can pretty much learn anything on there. Oh, I know! You should do a channel and give people like me some idea of how best to start off if they're interested in confectionery." The idea took root as I said it.

"I'm not sure—"

"You'd be great at it. You're a very good teacher." His brow arched. "You are. It was just that I'd already

158

done that stuff that you showed me a hundred times before. But for a complete novice, you'd be a dream come true."

Garrett's face turned a delightful shade of pink, and he picked up his spoon, indicating for me to eat my dessert. I was about to do just that when I heard a familiar voice I'd hoped never to hear again. "Do you need to make a show of me after I've gone to all this effort to treat you to an expensive meal?" the strident voice said, way too loud for a fancy restaurant.

It couldn't be, could it? Would Davey travel hundreds of miles out of his way to take someone to dinner? My heart sank, recalling he'd done exactly that before. Trepidation holding my full stomach hostage, I half-lifted out of my seat to peek past the floral arrangement. Sweat gathered at the base of my spine as I spotted Davey four tables over. He was sat with a guy who was sporting a look I was all too familiar with—fear.

"What, or who, are you looking at?" Garrett questioned, twisting to look over his shoulder, his view of the room a little less obscured than mine was.

Should I say something? The decision was taken from me when Davey chose that moment to look over in our direction. Fuck!

I sank back into my seat, hoping the guy would get lost. I held my breath as the seconds ticked by, convinced that my heart had stopped. Davey appeared at the table, glowering at us, Garrett looking up at him while I hoped like hell that I'd suddenly become invisible. Only that didn't happen, Davey getting in my face and growling, "You ungrateful little shit. Thought you could throw me aside for something better, did you?" His face held an ugly sneer as he glanced in Garrett's direction before dismissing him to turn his attention back to me.

"Something like that," I mumbled, feeling like I might be sick all over the pretty dessert I still hadn't touched.

Fingers dug painfully into the arm he'd broken. I winced, trying to draw my arm back, only to find it released suddenly as Garrett stood so fast that his seat tipped over and crashed to the floor. He gripped Davey's suit jacket and hauled him up in the air until his feet were dangling in mid-air. I was sure that my mouth must have been hanging open as Garrett shook Davey hard enough for his teeth to rattle. "Who are you, and why do you think it's okay to manhandle my boyfriend?"

The fluttering in my chest increased. I couldn't have said whether it was from fright, or from the way Garrett had emphasized the words "my boyfriend."

Davey scowled. "He was my boyfriend until he ran away in the middle of the night with all my money."

The outrageous lie left me speechless. During the four years I'd been with Davey, he'd never once put his hand in his pocket for anything. I'd paid my way and worked my ass off in his store. Now, he was accusing me of stealing!

The expression Garrett wore left me unable to work out what he'd made of Davey's accusation. He let go of Davey as the head waiter came over, lines of concern etched into his face.

The cute blond who'd previously been sitting with Davey also appeared, looking like he might piss himself at any moment. I missed what Garrett said to the waiter as I stood, squeezing past the table to avoid Davey, who thankfully had stopped paying me any attention as he ranted about Garrett's behavior.

I had one goal: save the poor sap stood hopping nervously from one foot to the other. I took hold of his arm and dragged him to the entrance of the restaurant. The second we were outside, I dropped his arm and started speaking. "You need to get as far away from Davey as you can. If he hasn't already laid into you, then it won't be long before he does. Then he'll start with the threats to your family. He's the biggest bastard I know, and a leopard never changes its spots."

The guy started to blubber in earnest. "He says if I leave, he'll find me and—"

"Yeah, I know the drill. Listen, he's violent and it only gets worse. Do you have a phone?" When he nodded, I held out my hand. "Give it me. I'll put my number in it. Call me when you know it's safe and I'll help you."

He did as I asked, his tear-drenched eyes reflecting confusion. "Why are you doing this? You don't even know me."

"I was you." I added the phone number for my apartment, my cell phone, and Ollie's just for good measure. Quickly returning the phone, I kept my eye on the restaurant door, knowing it wouldn't be long before Garrett and Davey came looking for us.

Only when the guy had his phone tucked back into the pocket of his pants, did I breathe a little easier.

"Wipe your face. You know he'll get madder than a hornet's nest if he sees you crying."

The guy shuddered and scrubbed at his face. His red, puffy eyes gave him away, but there was nothing I could do about that. "I'm Leeson by the way."

For the first time since I'd met the cute little twink, his lips trembled into a sweet smile, one that made my heart ache for what he must have been through with Davey.

"I'm Vic. Thank you for being nice to me. I don't know many people—"

He got no further as the door opened and Garrett appeared with Davey hot on his heels. "I'm pressing charges. There are witnesses to the fact you manhandled me."

"Fuck off! You laid your hands on my boyfriend. Do it again and it won't be him that ends up with a broken arm," Garrett growled menacingly, my cock taking more than a little notice.

Sick. You're one sick puppy!

My cock though, wasn't in agreement. I swallowed a sigh as I tucked the arm in question through Garrett's, completely ignoring Davey. "Let's go."

"You owe me," Davey shouted as we retreated.

Blood boiling with injustice, I let go of Garrett. I sent up a silent prayer that I wasn't about to make things worse for Vic, but I wasn't going to take Davey's shit anymore. "Listen here, dickweed. What I owe you is a broken arm, and more bruises than you can count. I never took a fucking dime from you. All that I took was control over my life back."

162

At the sound of clapping. I glanced over at Garrett, who grinned and continued to clap. "I want to go home," I said, flustered and more than ready to stop breathing the same air as Davey. He'd taken the shine off what had been, at least up until his unexpected appearance, the most perfect night of my life.

Shitty bastard. I hope he rots in hell!

18
Garrett

"Why do you look so grumpy this morning? I thought after last night you'd be all... relaxed and rejuvenated?" Jen was about as subtle as a sledgehammer as she winked at me.

"Seriously, how are we related?" I walked away from her, not in the mood for her antics, or for anything else at the moment. It was Leeson's day off, and after meeting Davey last night he'd insisted I drop him home. Ever since then I'd alternated between raging fury and sadness when I thought about what he'd endured at the hands of that asshole.

As I entered the office I went to shut the door, Jen barging in behind me before I could. "What gives? You had all these romantic plans last night. Yet, you look like someone stole one of your recipes."

I heaved out a sigh as I sat, burying my hands in my hair and yanking. "Lee's abusive and violent ex was in the restaurant with his latest victim. He spotted Lee and came over to the table, and tried to get a little handsy with him."

"For real? Oh my God! I hope you kicked the fucker in the balls and lodged them in the back of his throat."

Even as I winced at how descriptive she'd been, the laughter burst out of me. I might have wanted to do that very thing, but I didn't need the visual. "I didn't, but I gave him a fucking good shake, and while Lee was trying to rescue the guy Davey was with, I might have threatened him."

Jen's hands fisted and went to her hips. "Threatened him! You should have knocked out the guy's veneers."

"As much as that would have been gratifying, I'm not lowering myself to the same level of violence the guy likes to dish out. Firstly, that feeling would only last as long as it took to punch his fucking lights out. Secondly, there were witnesses, and he was already threatening to sue me. And lastly, Lee's been party to enough violence. I don't want him to think that I'm anything like Davey."

Jen came over and crouched down in front of me. "He knows that your bark is much worse than your bite. He never once cringes away from you when you start growling. Hell, I'd go as far as to say that he seems to get off on it, judging from the amount of times the pair of you go toe to toe."

The knots inside me from last night eased a little as it sank in that she was right. I hadn't wanted to acknowledge my concern that Lee had wanted to go home because of my behavior, but that didn't mean it didn't exist. "He chose to go home last night. I'm not sure why. I thought maybe it was because I'd got a little heavy-handed with his ex," I confessed.

"Nope, I bet he was majorly pissed that the guy ruined the night he'd planned." Jen slapped her hand over her mouth.

"What did he plan? He'd already shown me what he made for me." I gave Jen a searching look. "What am I missing here?"

She stood, fiddling with the strings of her apron that she always tied at the front. "It's… you… were, you know, taking it all slow and–"

"Stop right there! Nope. You are not going to talk about me and Lee… doing stuff."

"Jeez, how did I end up with a brother who is such a prude? Lee wanted the night to end with a–"

I shot out of the chair and, for my own sanity, covered her mouth to stop her from finishing the sentence. "I told you to shut up. What Lee and I do together is none of your business. Get that into your thick skull." I tapped on her head with the knuckles of my other hand. "You do not get to know the details of what Lee and I get up to."

She mumbled from behind my hand, "From what Lee has said, that would be nothing."

I rolled my eyes heavenward and dropped my hand from her mouth. "Give me strength. I was trying to get to know him. You know, have a conversation, learn what he likes and dislikes. It's how normal people date," I gritted out through clenched teeth.

"Brother, how long has it been since you dated? A decade! Now, it's all about learning how compatible you are in the bedroom before you get to the boring stuff." She shook her head, appearing genuinely mystified by my behavior.

Doubt started to creep in, making me wonder whether I'd really been doing the right thing in trying to learn more about Leeson before taking things further.

You've already had your tongue in his ass! "Oh, shut up!"

"It's the truth," Jen responded, making me realize I'd spoken aloud.

"Then what do you suggest I do?" The second her lips parted, I recognized the error of my ways. "No, don't tell me. I don't want to know."

She laughed. "You put tab A into slot B and then—"

"Get out, go... Go to LA. Maybe then I'll get some peace."

She laughed some more as she turned to open the door, pausing to look back at me. "You'll still miss me."

She wasn't wrong, but I wasn't about to tell her that. "Like a hole in the head," I fired back at her as she disappeared through the door. I rubbed at my face. What was I going to do about Leeson? Should I go over and... No, you're at work!

Given where my thoughts were heading, my cock had started to plump. I checked the time. It was still morning and I had a list of things to tackle. Fuck it! I got up, walking back into the kitchen and spending the next ten minutes cleaning everything up I'd brought to start cooking. Once it was sorted, I walked through the store, sending Jen a "don't you dare say a word" glare as I stomped past her before heading up the stairs to my apartment.

By the time I'd showered and changed into jeans and a button down, it was close to lunchtime. Once I was out in the street, I headed for the market, picking up several things that didn't require cooking before driving the six blocks to Leeson's apartment.

It was only as I stood outside the door that I remembered that with Ollie still having his leg in plaster he might be there too. It would seem that he was equally as clumsy as Leeson was. There was no point in not following through with my plan, though. I knocked, waiting for a minute before knocking again. Shit! Had Leeson gone out? Why hadn't I thought of that?

I shifted the bag of groceries to the opposite hand so I could pull my phone out and give Leeson a call to see if he was going to be back any time soon. I paused as the door opened a tiny crack. A pair of emerald eyes squinted at me before the door opened fully, Leeson giving me a relieved smile.

"Oh, thank God it's you. I was tempted not to open the door. I was half expecting it to be Davey. I know he has no idea where I live, but ever since I gave the apartment phone number to Vic, I've been expecting Davey to discover it and somehow figure out where I live. It wasn't the brightest of moves. I only figured it out in the car when we were heading home. Ollie's been a wreck all night, and it's all my fault. He hates confrontation of any kind."

Any doubts I still had about why Leeson had chosen to come home disappeared as he babbled. "Why didn't you say something last night?"

His lips puffed out as he looked at the floor. "I'd already ruined the night. The last thing you needed was to have to play bodyguard. You didn't sign up for that crap."

I struggled to contain my frustration as I dropped the bag on the floor to tug a sheepish-looking Leeson into my arms. "Now listen up, and listen good. I've signed up for whatever being a part of your life involves. There aren't any exceptions. None. Got it?"

He blinked slowly, his Adam's apple bobbing as he nodded. "Got it."

"Good! Now, I've brought some things to make a kind of table picnic lunch. You want to share it with me?"

His lips formed into a breath-taking smile. "Yes please, but have you got enough for Ollie too?" He glanced at the bag sitting at our feet.

"There is. But after we've eaten, I'd like to go someplace to... have some alone time." I stressed the last part, hoping he'd understand that meant him naked, and me doing all the things I'd hoped to do the night before.

He bobbed his head in agreement so fast that he looked like his neck was on a spring. I chuckled, giving him a quick kiss before releasing him so that I could grab the bag. "Show me to your kitchen."

When we got to the kitchen, I stared at in disbelief. "How on earth did you create that masterpiece in this... kitchen? If you can even call it that."

Ollie, who had appeared at our side, giggled. "You've no idea how creative he gets in here."

The space was about two foot by three. It was so small that it would have been a struggle to swing a cat. It had none of the equipment I used, and I shuddered at the sight of the few items scattered across the counter.

"I'm used to it. I've got into the habit of making do with what's available." Lee gave a shrug as if it meant nothing, taking the bag from my hands and opening it to pull out the contents.

He was a fucking miracle worker. "How has no one ever seen how talented you are before?"

His gaze remained on the food he was arranging "I kept it to myself. Well, except for Ollie. My mom, my dad, and my brothers and sister know I like to dabble. But I never talk about my dreams 'cause I don't want my family to feel bad. There was never going to be enough money for school or for the things I'd have needed."

Although he was giving out the vibe that it didn't matter, it clearly did from the way his eyes shone when he chanced a glance in my direction.

"I'm going to do everything in my power to make sure you get to live your dream." I meant it, every damn word, and I'd do it, even if it was the last thing I did.

Ollie sniffed, breaking the tension that had been crackling between us, Leeson's eyes going wide. "We going to eat that food or just stare at it?" Ollie asked as he hobbled past me to get to the counter where the food was.

"Yeah, let's eat." Leeson gave me a bright, shimmering smile as he reached up to a cupboard to retrieve three plates.

Once the food had been demolished and Ollie had been dropped off at the art store where he'd worked before falling, I drove back to Sweet Haven in silence with Leeson next to me. He spent most of the time staring out of the window while he played with the edge of his seatbelt.

Was he nervous about what was going to happen? It wasn't very spontaneous, was it? Unlike the spanking, which had been a spur of the moment thing. I mentally

171

slapped my own forehead at my lack of finesse. It all felt a bit odd and awkward now that we were alone.

"We don't have to go to the apartment. We could go for… a walk?"

He twisted around in his seat to put a hand on my thigh, making it difficult to keep my eyes on the road. "No, I want to go to the apartment, if you do?"

He sounded so nervous that I risked a glance in his direction. "What's troubling you?"

As straightforward as ever, he answered, "Do you still want me after last night?"

"Fuck, yes. I thought we'd sorted this out back at your place. What I feel for you hasn't changed just because you have a dickweed ex. As you know, I have one of my own. Right now, all I want is to get some alone time that doesn't involve much talking and does involve lots of…"

Leeson groaned, the fingers pressing against my thigh digging in. "You need to stop or I'm not going to be decent enough to walk through the store."

I chanced another glance at him to find him staring at the obvious bulge in his jeans, laughter booming out of me at how put-out he appeared. "I've got a jacket you can put on to… hide your predicament."

"Oh, you think this is funny, do you?" As he spoke, his hand moved up my leg to stroke the junction between groin and thigh, his fingertips grazing my swelling cock.

He pressed a little more firmly and I started to hyperventilate. I indicated and slowed down, trying to get my head out of my pants and onto what I needed to do. "You're playing with fire," I growled as a gap appeared in the traffic, allowing me to turn down the street and park at the back of the store.

19

Leeson

The growly voice he was using only fueled the desire that had come from Garrett's honesty about wanting me, even more. After last night, when Garrett had driven off with no more than a distracted peck on the lips, I'd thought Davey had fucked things up for me. Now that that was no longer an issue, all I wanted was to get him naked and see just how creative he could get. The man's kisses could turn me into a horny, hot mess. And we'd done plenty of kissing since the spanking, but little else. I loved that he was trying to get to know me, I really did, but my cock was fed up with my own hand. It wanted more. It wanted Garrett.

As he parked up, I unclipped my seatbelt and dived on him. In my hurry, I banged my knee on the steering wheel. "Shit. Why do cars have to be so... confined," I complained, rubbing at my injured knee while still trying to crawl into Garrett's lap.

"What about we wait till we get inside? Where I have plenty of wide-open space to prevent you from hurting yourself."

He reached for the door as I laughed at the ridiculousness of his statement. "You do know me, right? I could hurt myself on air."

"Yes. Okay, I concede that fact, but maybe a big, comfy bed will help?" he offered with a hopeful smile glancing back at me as he got out of the car. "Are you coming?"

"Fuck no. But soon, I hope," I muttered under my breath as I turned to exit the car through my door, thinking it would be safer for both of us.

The walk through the kitchen, the store, and up the stairs felt like an eternity. I hadn't missed the high five Jen had offered to Nese as we'd walked through the store. Given Garrett's head shake, I figured he'd seen it too.

The key rattled in the lock for a second, Garrett opening the door and stepping aside to let me enter first. Not needing a second invitation, I strolled past him, my hands already tugging at my T-shirt. I sucked in a shaky breath, throwing caution to the wind and removing it in one fluid movement that was a lot more graceful than I normally was.

I turned to face Garrett, my hand lowering to my belt buckle. "I think you have far too many clothes on."

His brows rose and his nostrils flared as a deep flush appeared on his cheek bones. There was an intensity about him that I'd often witnessed when he was in full creative mode in the kitchen. It made my blood sing with excitement now that it was focused on me.

"Maybe you need to come here and do something about that," he growled.

Shivers ran over my bare skin as I finished unfastening my jeans and pushed them down my legs. Careful not to trip over my own feet, I stepped out of my sneakers before removing the rest of my clothes. Garrett's chest heaved as I stood tall—naked and aroused.

I opened my arms to him. "I think you should come and take what you want." The second he moved, I spun around, running out into the hallway which led to the bedroom. I entered his room a few seconds later, the fact I'd never snooped in there meaning that he caught me as I tried to get my bearings. His arms wrapped around my middle, lifting me off the carpeted floor and tossing me onto the huge queen-sized bed that dominated the room.

I bounced and landed in a heap, giggling.

"Right, now I've got you, what am I going to do with you?"

I rolled onto my back and gave him a cheeky grin. "I can think of several things. Only you need to be naked for them." I sat up, resting back on my elbows. "Want some help?"

"I think I've got it covered." He made a show out of taking his shoes, socks, and button down off. By which time there was a pool of pre-cum on my belly from the way his gaze continually roamed over me as he undressed.

My heated desire undermined any hope of pretending that this wasn't something monumental happening between us. Dreams of this moment paled in comparison next to the reality of the gorgeous man standing naked at the foot of the bed. Thick, dark hair covered his barrel chest, spreading down to his lower abdomen, his cock standing thick and proud from a thatch of bushy hair. I licked my lips, hoping I'd get the opportunity to bury my face in all of that lush hair.

He was a total unashamed bear, and I fucking loved it. His legs were as hairy as the rest of him, and I wanted to know how it felt to have those strong, hairy limbs wrapped around me.

"Do you like what you see?" he rasped as he finally climbed onto the bed.

"You are a total wet dream. The hair fuck it's my weakness. If you find me rubbing all over you, you're gonna have to just go with it."

He tilted his head back and roared with laughter in a way I hadn't witnessed before. The pure joy of it was wonderful. So much so that I joined in as he pulled me to him and pressed my cheek to his chest. Through his laughter, he said, "Rub away."

Taking him at his word, I pushed him down, waiting till he was stretched out on the bed. Only then did I crawl on top of him, pressing the whole of my body against his. The scent of musk filled my nose as I buried my face in his chest and inhaled. Overwhelmed by the feel of the soft hair stroking my skin, and his rich scent, I lay content in his arms as he held me close. His heartbeat thudded against my ear, my skin vibrating with the fast rhythm.

I wasn't sure how long we lay like that before I shifted to look into Garrett's hooded eyes. "Can I touch you?"

"Yes."

That one word held a wealth of power that he'd given over to me. I held his gaze as I lowered my head to kiss the place where his heart lay. His chest rose and fell in rapid succession, but he stayed silent as I encouraged him to part his thighs so that

178

I could sit between them. His cock was as hard as mine but I ignored it for now, rising to my haunches so that I could reach his chest and run my fingers over the hairy wall of muscle, the action producing a moan.

The dark discs nestled in the hair called to me. I made a show of wetting the tips of my fingers, gently circling the pebbled flesh until both buds stood proud. My pre-cum dripped onto Garrett and he groaned, his hips lifting until his hard length caressed mine.

I sucked in a shaky breath, tutting and sitting back even though it was the last thing I wanted to do. "You said I could touch you, so behave and let me."

"I was helping."

My lips twitched. "Help a little less, or this will be over before its even started."

"I don't see a problem with that."

His raspy voice made shivers run down my spine, my willpower disintegrating. I moved, straddling his hips so that I could rest my ass on his hard length. I gave my hips a little swivel, rewarded by a low growl, his cock pulsing and pre-cum smearing my balls. "You leave me no choice. When I was bad, you disciplined me." I licked my lower lip and then tapped it, hoping to provoke him. "How do you propose that I punish you?" I rolled my hips again, his cock nestling deeper in the crease of my backside. The heat and proximity to my hole did all sorts of things to the need inside me that was clawing to be set free.

He rolled, the movement as fast as lightning. I landed on my back, the air leaving my body as he gave me a sexy sneer. "Now let's talk about punishments. Do you think it's nice to tease me like that?"

He gave me no time to answer before his mouth claimed mine. It was all heat and desperation, his tongue seeking entry into my mouth and overpowering me with desire. The kiss was wet and more than a little out of control as we rolled, our lips never parting. Every inch of my flesh was on fire from the feel of the silky hair brushing against me. I doubted electrocution could have made me feel more. This was everything. My pulse pounded in my ears from lack of oxygen, but the last thing I wanted was for him to stop.

His hands seemed to be everywhere at once and I gloried in his loss of control. "Lube... condoms... we need..." He didn't finish, his mouth claiming mine again, his hands gripping my ass cheeks and digging in hard, but not hard enough to bruise. It was perfect. He flipped me again until I was back on top of him. "Reach into the bedside drawer," he gasped against my wet lips.

I reached out blindly, and there was a loud crash as something smashed on the floor. Garrett chuckled. "I was wrong, even in my bed you're clumsy."

I sat up, my chest heaving as I glanced to the place where there'd once been a lamp before looking back at Garrett, who was grinning foolishly at me. I jabbed at his chest. "It's your fault for not getting the supplies ready before we started. And you were kissing me, distracting me from what I was doing." I tried to sound affronted. Only it came out all giggly instead.

He lay a hand on his forehead, his dramatic sigh increasing my laughter. "You saw through my dastardly plan."

I slapped his chest before reaching toward the drawer he'd indicated to find what we needed. I held up the condom and lube and gave him a wicked smile. "I guess I get to decide who wears them."

He stilled, his cock seeming to grow harder against me, his eyes glowing in a way that made it hard to swallow. I'd only been joking but if I wasn't mistaken, he liked the idea of me topping. "Are you versatile?" I held my breath.

"I like the idea of you fucking me, so I suppose I must be. My previous partners were all more interested in me fucking them."

He didn't seem particularly comfortable talking about it, so I let it go for now, promising myself I'd return to the subject later. "I think that's something we can explore another time. 'Cause right now all I want is to feel your cock inside me." I ground down hard on his cock, getting a long, low groan for my efforts.

"Damn, if I don't want that too."

Without saying anything else I rose up, moving back so that I had better access to his slick cock. The head gleamed in the afternoon sun coming through the bedroom windows. I bent forward and slid my tongue over the tip, wanting to taste. Only from the moment I touched him, I couldn't seem to stop, dropping what I held to free up my hands. I sucked the head between my lips and swirled my tongue over the mushroom head. His hips rose, and I changed position to allow myself to take him a little deeper.

Suctioning my cheeks, I took another couple of inches into my mouth, his girth stretching my mouth wide. The rich scent of his musk grew stronger the closer my nose got to his groin. The musk that must have been in his body wash was even more evident as I inhaled, loving the combination of the fragrances. "You smell fucking amazing," I muttered around his cock, saliva dripping down my chin and pooling in the hair at the base. I ran my fingers through it, looking up to meet his heated gaze as I used wet fingers to go back and play with his nipple.

The second I pinched the hard bud, his hips rose again, his cock trying to punch a hole in my tonsils. I coughed and spluttered as I pulled back, spit dripping down my chin and onto my chest. I swiped at my chin, giving him a grin of pure devilment as I picked up the condom. Garrett growled as I fumbled with the wrapper, the sound making my hands shake even more. "Stop making noises like that. It isn't helping me."

He growled again, low and deep, as I rolled the condom down his shaft, making sure to tease him as I did so. Lube in hand, I climbed off his lap, turning my back on him and rising to my knees. I coated my fingers and then dropped the bottle. Glancing back over my shoulder, I used one hand to spread my ass cheeks and slipped lubed fingers close to my hole. Garrett's hand moved to his cock. He stroked himself as I slipped a finger past the tight rim of muscle and groaned at the feeling. It had been quite some time since I'd played with my ass and the burn was delicious.

Garrett never took his gaze off the hand playing with my ass. I shifted my thighs further apart and leant forward a little so that he could see the two fingers I now had stretching me. By the time I had three fingers inside me I was struggling not to come. As if sensing how close I was, Garrett rasped out, "Come here. Now."

I didn't hesitate, removing my fingers and spinning around. In my haste, I toppled forward, Garrett grunting as I landed on him.

He chuckled. "You should have a warning label attached." He lifted me to position me over his cock, my mouth drying up as he lowered me slowly.

My fingers dug into his chest and I panted at the warm pressure against my hole as he held me steady and rocked his hips slowly.

"Feels so good," I gasped out as he pushed the head of his cock inside me.

"Fuck, yeah!" Garrett's heavy-lidded gaze held me captive. Too many emotions to name, flitted across his face and I found that I couldn't breathe as he pushed deeper inside me, owning my heart in that moment.

Sweat slid down my face, my eyes stinging by the time my ass met his groin. The stretch was mind-blowing, but none of that mattered as Garrett stroked my arms. "You're so fucking beautiful."

The thickness in my throat made it difficult to respond, so I moved forward instead, groaning as his cock hit my prostate. Undeterred, I claimed his mouth, kissing him with all the feelings inside me that I couldn't voice.

He rocked his hips and I clung onto his shoulders, unwilling to release his lips. He started slowly at first, but that didn't last long, his cock hitting my prostate head-on, my cock howling for more as I ground against him.

There was the sound of flesh hitting flesh, as well as moans and groans. It was fucking intoxicating, the scent of sex permeating the warm air. Desperate to see his face, I pulled back to move seductively against him. On and on it went, sensation flooding my cock, the tingle alerting me that I was about to come. I reached down to stroke myself, my hand knocked away.

"Mine, God it's mine, let me make you come."

I nodded, throwing my head back and letting him take control. His hand stroked me, the rough callouses on his palms too much, and I roared, "I'm coming!"

Every part of me hummed with life and I lost all coordination, cum spurting over Garrett's hand and his hairy stomach. Still stroking my cock, he sat up, claiming my mouth as he thrust up hard enough for me to see stars, my cock making a concerted effort to keep offering up its prize.

"You feel so damn good. I don't want to stop, ever," Garrett panted against my mouth before kissing me again.

God, I wanted that. I never wanted to leave him. My heart tripped in my chest as he moaned into my mouth, his body going rigid as he came in the condom. I instantly regretted the use of the condom, but I bit back the complaint as Garrett flopped backwards on the bed, panting, with me clutched to his chest.

His body was soaked with sweat and cum, the hair on his chest damp and sticky. It felt a little strange as I nestled against him and buried my face in his chest. A sense of completeness I'd never experienced with anyone before swept over me. My slowing heart rate sped up again. Would Garrett be interested in more than a short-term thing with me?

"What's going on in your head?" Garrett questioned, his fingers threading though my hair.

I sucked in a breath and lifted up so that I could see his reaction. "What is it that we're doing? Are we just fuck buddies, or is it... more?"

"More. I've never done fuck buddies. Is that okay?"

"Yes, yes, a hundred times yes."

His cock slipped from my ass as he rolled me over and gave me his special smile. "Is it official then? Are we dating exclusively?"

"I'm pretty sure you called me your boyfriend yesterday, just sayin'"

"That I did. So, are we exclusive?" he asked again, a hint of something in his voice I couldn't interpret.

"We're exclusive. Me, you, and your kitchen appliances."

He shook his head and laughed again. It rumbled through his chest, making the damp hair rub against my bare skin. A shiver of pleasure ran through me.

"And my kitchen appliances," he muttered before kissing me.

20
Garrett

Ever since Leeson had spent the day in my bed three weeks ago, we'd been inseparable. I'd never thought of myself as clingy person, but Leeson had proved me wrong. It had taken me until the age of forty-one to discover someone I wanted to be close to without feeling like I needed alone time or space. It was... I wasn't sure what it was, but I wasn't complaining because he seemed to feel the same way.

He was currently stood to my left, his gaze fixed in front of him on the contents of the bowl he was stirring. The warm feeling that came from having him close had become more frequent, and it no longer scared me. If this was how it felt to be in a relationship with someone who understood who I was, then I never wanted it to end. My vow to never get into another serious relationship had been lost somewhere in the depth of feelings Leeson evoked in me. It was fucking wonderful. Leeson not only got me, but seemed attuned to my needs. When I was with him, and the creative urge to go into the kitchen struck, which could be any time of the day and night, he'd follow me and either do something himself or just sit and watch me work silently. Those times were precious, and no matter how focused I was on what I was doing, I always knew he was there. Again, this was new to me, and the more I thought about it, the more I understood that it had always been that way ever since he'd first stepped into my kitchen and my life.

This guy was the perfect match I'd never known I wanted or needed. There was no comparison to what I'd shared with Teddy, a fact that left me with all sorts of mixed emotions. I was devastated that I'd wasted all those years, but without them I'd probably never have appreciated Leeson for the person he was.

"Can you run through that recipe again? I missed what you did at the end." Leeson looked down at my bowl and then back at his own. "Mine is a funny color." He scowled as he pushed his bowl away.

"I thought you were paying attention?"

"I was. It's just that when you get all silent and broody with that intense look on your face, my cock seems to think it's time to play."

He sounded so serious that I did a double-take. My gaze narrowed on him. "You're messing with me, aren't you?" I glanced around the kitchen to check we were alone.

Leeson had no such boundaries when he was horny, taking hold of my hand and pressing it to his arousal. I exhaled sharply, stroking down his hard shaft without any prompting. Wanting his cock in my hand, I pulled at the waistband of his chef's pants, pleased that they were elasticated and therefore allowed me easy access.

His breath came in short pants as I took a firm hold of his cock and lazily stroked him from base to tip, gathering pre-cum to aid the glide of my hand.

"This is a professional kitchen," he grunted, mimicking what I often said to him, his hips rocking into each stroke.

"Is that so? Aren't I being professional by offering my work colleague a helping hand?" I whispered into his ear. I licked at it, enjoying the way he shuddered, and the tiny whimpering sounds he made.

"You'll make me come if you carry on doing that." The words were said in barely more than a choked-out whisper, but not once did Leeson try and remove my hand.

I couldn't quite believe my own behavior. Leeson was such a bad influence on me. He really was. Yeah, it's all his fault you put your hand in his pants!

I chuckled at the snarky voice as I kept on doing what I'd never have done in a million years with Teddy.

"I want you to come. Right now, in the kitchen. I want to know that every time you work next to me at this counter, you'll be thinking of my hand touching you."

"Argh fuckkkkk!" He cried out, his cock thickening and his hips juddering as cum coated my fingers and his underwear.

He looked so utterly dazed and flushed by the time he'd finished mewling that I had to kiss him. Claiming his mouth, I lost myself in the sweet taste of him, my cock aching with the need to be buried balls deep inside him. It seemed in my efforts to tease him that I'd done the same to myself.

"I love you," he gasped out. He froze, his mouth remaining open as I pulled back so as not to spook him.

His eyes were as huge as saucers, consuming his whole face.

"Do you mean it?" Fuck, I hoped he meant it. Please don't take it back.

Neither of us seemed to care that my hand was still down his pants as we stood staring at each other. I couldn't fathom out what he was thinking, emotions passing across his face too quickly before they were gone.

"Fuck, yeah I do. I know it seems rushed but, hell." He ran his hands through his hair, finally shifting enough that I had to remove my sticky hand from his pants. He gave a sigh as he eyed my hand. "It's not that my head is full of sexy time, okay. Though it is, and that was a fucking mind-blowing orgasm, but it's more than that," he waffled, going a beautiful shade of pink.

"Glad we've cleared that up." My lips twitched at the way he rolled his eyes heavenward before he stomped over to the sink and grabbed a cloth, returning with it.

"Here, wipe your hand. I can't concentrate with you covered in my cum."

"Covered in what?" Jen screeched from the doorway.

Fuck!

A wave of heat rode up my face so fast that I wasn't sure there was anywhere left on my body that wasn't red. I heaved out a sigh as I wiped my hand on the cloth Leeson had given me, trying to hide the evidence of what had just happened. "Nothing, just–"

"Hey, this is me you're talkin' to. The pair of you have been all over each other every second you can. But seriously, please tell me you didn't do the nasty right here?"

Did I detect a hint of pride in her reaction? I worked hard to maintain my composure under her scrutiny.

"No, we didn't do the nasty in the kitchen," Leeson lied, or semi-lied, because I was sure that a hand job, even if it had been inside his pants broke several hygiene codes.

I took the cloth Leeson had given me and threw it in the wastepaper bin before going over to the sink to wash my hands. Jen was still standing in the doorway, her gaze moving between myself and Leeson. He appeared to be struggling not to fidget, his hands fluttering at his sides. I had to bite my lower lip to keep my laughter contained. Laughing wasn't going to make the situation any better, that was for sure.

"Now your hands are clean, can I have another tray of the berry cream candy we've run out of?" Jen gave us both a hard stare and left as silently as she'd arrived.

Leeson pointed at me. "The blame for this sits squarely on your shoulders. If you hadn't started with all that sexy talk"—he waved his hands in the air before pointing to his groin— "I wouldn't have underwear full of cum." The latter was whispered as he gave a furtive glance at the door.

"How can it be my fault when you're so damn irresistible," I replied grumpily, trying to recall what it was I'd been doing when all I wanted to do was talk about Leeson's confession.

Had he said it in the heat of the moment, or did he really mean it? Wasn't it too soon? We'd known each other less than two months. Was it possible to develop feelings that weren't just lust in that time? What I'd felt for Teddy in the beginning had been lust—pure and simple. We might not have rushed into stuff, but it was definitely fucking that had been on my mind. With Leeson, although getting naked was fun, it wasn't everything. We spent a lot of time out of the bedroom laughing, watching movies, and figuring out new recipes to try together. He challenged me and made me think outside the box, which in turn stimulated me in ways I hadn't been since the beginning of my career. He didn't want to compete with me, and that was the thing that really got my juices flowing.

"Are you going to brood, or are you going to talk to me?"

Something else I... loved about him was that he never let me hide from what was going on in my head. I put down the spoon I'd just picked up and turned to face him. He was chewing on his lower lip, but there was a challenge in his eyes to match the question.

Knowing it would rile him, I scowled. "I'm not brooding. How many times do I have to tell you that?"

"Really? You're the king of broodiness. Oh, and don't forget grumpiness. That has to be on the list." He stepped closer, narrowing the distance between us. "But, I'm on to you. Are you going to avoid talking about the fact that I said I loved you?" His voice quivered, but he continued to meet my gaze.

There was a buzzing in my ears as I gently cupped his bristly cheeks and bent over until my lips were a mere inch from his. "I love you. I think you stole my heart the second you told me that I'd burnt the chocolate."

His breath brushed my lips as he giggled. "It was burnt, and I was so disappointed to find that my hero was just as fallible as the rest of us. It was an epic fall off the pedestal I'd put you on." He ended his speech with a dramatic sigh.

My lips twitched, a grin spreading across my face. "I'll have to see what I can do to regain my position." I kissed his lips softly, swallowing his whimper before easing back before we had a repeat of earlier. "Now, shall we see where you went wrong?"

He blinked twice, the smile on his face leaving my heart swelling in my chest. "How could I have gone wrong when I've got you?"

How could I argue with that logic?

21

Leeson

The chime of my phone drew my attention to the table where it sat. I retrieved it as Ollie appeared to look at the screen over my shoulder. "Who's Vic?"

"The guy I told you about who was unfortunate enough to get mixed up with Davey." I opened the message that started with, *Hi this is Vic*, the air becoming trapped in my chest as I read the rest of it.

Did you mean what you said about helping me? I'm in pretty bad shape and really need somewhere safe to hide out. Please help. I've got no one else to turn to.

"He sounds desperate," I said, looking up into Ollie's equally concerned gaze. "We need to help him."

Ollie glanced around our small apartment. "There isn't much room here. I mean he could crash on the sofa, but that will only work for so long."

I swallowed hard. "I've been meaning to talk to you about..." I trailed off, searching for the best way of bringing up that Garrett had broached the subject of me moving in with him. I'd been stewing over it for the last couple of weeks, wanting to see how things progressed between us since blurting out my true feelings. I'd been on the cusp of declaring my feelings more than a dozen times before that and he'd finally caught me at a moment of weakness. Then I hadn't wanted to take it back, not when he'd looked so damn hopeful. I'd been left floating somewhere in the clouds when he'd confessed his own feelings.

The thing was, I was practically living with him anyway. I was only home today because I'd taken Ollie for his final check-up with the orthopedic surgeon. The plaster had been replaced three weeks ago with a walking boot, allowing him to walk on it for short periods of time. It was now down to physiotherapy to strengthen the weakened muscles. Ollie could return to work in the gallery as long as he didn't stand for long periods of time, which his boss was more than happy with. It seemed chaos had ruled while Ollie hadn't been there.

"You've got that look on your face that says I'm not going to like what you're going to say." Ollie pointed a finger at me. "Spit it out before it chokes you."

"I've decided to move in with Garrett. I know it's fast but, hell, I'm already living there. Please don't be mad at me."

Ollie sighed. "I figured this was coming. At least you waited till I could afford to pay the rent." He came over to give me a warm hug. "I'll miss you. But I suppose at least it means that this Vic can have your room."

He sounded more resigned than happy, so I gave him hard squeeze. "I can tell Vic, no."

"Don't be silly. There's no way I can let you do that. I saw what Davey was capable of first-hand. We need to help. I just hope he hasn't got any annoying habits or anything."

I chuckled, giving Ollie another hug before looking back at the message. "Do you think I should just ring him? This number will come up on his screen, so if he's scared to answer that should help. What do you think?"

I continued to dither, Ollie snatching the phone out of my hand and pressing dial. He put it on speaker, the dialing tone loud as we waited to see if Vic would answer.

"Hello, Lee? is that you?" said the frightened-sounding voice.

Ollie's eyes gleamed with unshed tears as he gulped, nodding at me to answer.

"Yes, it is. Where are you? Do you need me to come and get you?" My mind was already racing with thoughts of how I could do that without a car.

There was a shuddery intake of breath. "Where are you?"

I glanced at Ollie, praying that Davey wasn't trying to set me up by using Vic. When he nodded, I said, "I'm in Sweet Haven. Do you know where that is?"

"I do. I went through the town once with a friend. I'm about a hundred or so miles from there. I can get a bus. Will you be able to meet me when I arrive? I'm not sure I can walk far." His voice broke on a sob, Ollie's lips trembling.

"Are you alright to travel? I can come to you if you need me to." I'd ask Garrett if I could borrow his car if I needed to. I was sure he'd say yes.

"I'm already at the bus depot as I've just got off the bus that left town. No, it's best if I get the bus. I don't want to hang around here any longer than I have to... you know, just in case he's following me."

"Ring me when you get close, and I'll make sure I'm where I need to be."

The call ended quickly after that. "He sounds in a bad way," Ollie said, fretting as he started to hobble back and forth.

"Yeah, he does. But let's not stress too much until we see him and know what Davey has done to him." I pocketed my phone. "I think I'm gonna head to the store and ask Garrett if I can borrow his car."

For the first time since Vic had answered the phone, Ollie gave me a weak smile. "I'm coming with you, if only to watch you wheedle the car keys off Garrett."

My grumpy bear was far from tamed, but then I didn't want that. Fuck no! I loved him all growly. But he smiled and laughed more, a fact Jen never failed to point out to him, which just made him even grumpier. It was a win-win situation.

We got a cab so that Ollie didn't need to walk, arriving ten minutes later at the store. A smile spread across my face at the large queue, both inside and outside the store. Every day that passed, there seemed to be more people turning up who I'd never seen before.

Word was getting out and I even had some requests for special orders and I'd talked Garrett into producing some of his cartoon chocolate figures.

The one he'd made of me for Valentine's Day had been so good that I'd refused to eat it. I'd gotten a clear plastic, airtight box to keep it in. All

Garrett had done was roll his eyes at me, but I think he was secretly pleased that I loved it so much.

Jen gave me a pleading look as we entered the store. "Can you give me and Nese a hand to serve some of these customers?"

I nodded. "Give me two minutes to wash my hands and grab an apron." I glanced at Ollie. "You could help by manning the cash register."

He gave a shrug. "If you want. I'll need something to perch on, though."

"I'll grab a stool from Garrett's apartment. I'm sure he won't mind."

The man himself appeared through the open door behind the counter, a big beaming smile on his face. "I thought I heard you. What won't I mind?"

Jen nudged him out of the way as she went over to the next customer, who was too busy staring at Garrett to take any notice of the fact that Jen was talking to him. Jealousy nipped at me as I walked around the counter to tug on Garrett's apron and lay claim to his mouth in a hot, wet kiss.

His chest heaved, his breathing as erratic as if he'd been jogging. "Now what did I do to deserve that?" His brows rose as he glanced back at the store full of customers.

Shit, had I just fucked up?

He flicked the end of my nose, the kiss that followed on the same spot, allaying any concerns I might have had before it took hold. "What do you need?"

"If I said that aloud, I'd probably get arrested. So, I'll go with one of your kitchen stools for Ollie to sit on."

A female voice shouted, "Spoilsport," twitters of laughter making Garrett's face glow. He bent down to whisper in my ear, "You're gonna find your backside red later."

I squirmed, avoiding eye contact with everyone as I scuttled over to the door which led up to the apartment. When I returned, Garrett had disappeared, the queue not quite as long as it had been before.

Three hours passed before my phone rang. By which time the mad rush in the store was over. Jen and Nese had gone to grab a quick drink, leaving me and Ollie manning the store.

"When Jen leaves, how will Nese cope on her own?" Ollie asked as I pulled my phone out to look at the screen.

He was right. Nese wasn't going to cope on her own, but I didn't have any answers for him at the moment, not with my mind so full of what I was about to be confronted with when I answered the phone. Pressing the button to answer, I asked without preamble, "Vic, you nearly in town?"

"About ten minutes out. The bus stop is on the main street before he heads to the depot. The driver mentioned several other stops before that, but I can't remember them. I'm sorry."

"It's all good. The store I work in is on the main street so that's perfect. I'll head to the bus stop and wait for you."

Ollie limped over to stand next to me. The second I ended the call, he said, "I'm coming with you."

"Fine. Just let me tell the others we're leaving."

22

Garrett

For what felt like the hundredth time, I looked out into the store to see if Leeson had returned with the guy we'd met at the restaurant. I got why he'd offered to help, but that didn't mean I had to like it. This Davey character was a loose cannon, and I didn't want him anywhere near Leeson. Fuck, no.

"Big brother, what is it? You're acting like you've got ants in those expensive pants of yours."

"Have you seen Lee?"

"It's the same answer I gave you the last dozen times you asked. Do I need to say it again?"

Nese laughed before continuing to chat with the guy who looked more interested in her than in buying anything. If I wasn't mistaken, this was his third visit in the last week. "Why do you have to be such a smart ass?" I gave her a forced smile.

"Because I learnt from the best."

The door opened, the air disappearing from the room. Vic, stood, or more precisely sagged between Ollie and Leeson. He looked as if he'd been knocked over by a bus. His face was swollen and bore an array of dark-colored bruises. His head was so swollen that it looked a little misshapen, and there were fingerprint bruises circling what I could see of his neck. What the fuck had that monster done to him?

I walked around the counter to where the men had stopped. "Let me help. Do you need to go to the hospital?" Ollie and Leeson relinquished the hold they had on the battered man and I carefully slid my arm around his back, at the same time as putting an arm under his legs to scoop him up.

"No," Vic whispered, cringing in my arms.

"I promise I'm not going to hurt you." The man talking to Nese stared as I headed in their direction.

"I can help." His assessing gaze ran over Vic. "I'm a trained paramedic."

Vic started to sob, but I nodded. "Follow me." I went through the door and straight up the stairs, not stopping until I'd reached the top. Leeson was closest to me. I glanced at him. "Can you dig my keys out, or better yet use your own to open the door?"

He edged past us, careful not to knock Vic in my arms. Once the door was open, I headed straight for the sofa and laid him down. The paramedic immediately dropped to his haunches and started to fire off questions. He seemed legit as he examined Vic.

Leeson wrapped his arms around my waist and I held him tight, resting my chin on top of his head. How had he lived with this kind of violence? A shudder ran through me as the man got Vic to pull up his top to reveal his chest. There didn't appear to be any part that wasn't marred with ugly bruising. "That fucking monster!"

"Yes, he is. He has to pay for this," Leeson whispered brokenly. "If I'd reported him instead of running, Vic might not be in this state," he sobbed into my chest.

Emotion made it impossible to speak or swallow, a fact only made worse as Vic started to retell the horror of the last few days.

When the guy examining him finally stood, his mouth was set in a grim line. "I think he's got a couple of broken ribs." He glanced back to Vic, who was lying still with his eyes shut. "He needs to go to hospital, even if it's only to get pain meds and his ribs strapped."

"I don't have insurance," he mumbled, his eyes staying closed as tears dripped down his mottled skin.

"It's fine, I'll cover the cost. All you need to worry about is healing, and then kicking Davey's ass," I gritted out through clenched teeth, struggling to keep my own emotions in check.

Tear-drenched eyelashes flickered open to reveal a depth of despair that made me determined to hold on to the rage flowing through me like molten lava. How could someone do this to another human being and think it was okay? The fact that in the past it had been Leeson in the same situation made it that much more real, my heart cut to shreds.

"I might not be able to pay you back."

"We'll figure it out. Right now, we need to get you to the hospital, and on the mend. The rest can wait till later."

I glanced at the paramedic who was standing silently watching our exchange. "Can you get an ambulance to come and take him to the hospital?"

"That won't be a problem." The guy dug into the pocket of his jeans as he walked off and disappeared through my front door.

My apartment became a hive of activity after that, two paramedics arriving and doing their own assessment of Vic before carefully lifting him onto a stretcher and carrying him to the ambulance. Leeson insisted on going with Vic, and I didn't argue. Whereas Ollie opted to go home, Jen offering to drive him once she'd closed the store.

An hour later I stood in my kitchen, staring blindly at the full counter as I tried to get the images of Vic out of my head, my fingers tingling as I recalled tracing the bumps on Leeson's left arm.

He'd told me what I was sure was an abbreviated version of the night Davey had broken his arm to the degree where he'd had a bone poking through the skin. What had he called it? A compound fracture, that was it. He'd needed an operation to fix the bone and remove the splinters. It was while he was in hospital that he'd come to the decision to call Davey's bluff about the threats he'd made.

The fucker was a bully and coward, who'd clearly never had his ass handed to him by someone bigger and stronger than he was. The sound of dishes hitting the floor had me blinking at the mess I'd made. "Fucking hell," I growled, eyeing the state of the kitchen before grabbing a broom to sweep up the mess before Leeson returned.

I'd never been one to think that violence was the answer, but I was struggling to see straight with the anger boiling inside me. The burning need to hunt Davey down and teach him a lesson he'd never forget stole the breath from my lungs. My chest burned, my hands shaking from the violent urges running through me as I held the broom.

You need to calm the fuck down. You're no good to Leeson like this. He doesn't need this. He doesn't need to see you like this. I tried to listen to the voice of reason, but it was a close call which was going to win as it battled with the anger. I closed my eyes, squeezing them tight in an effort to block out the images which continued to plague me.

Think about Leeson's smile. Think, for fuck's sake.

Little by little, I reined myself in until I could breathe without my chest hurting. I didn't know how much time had passed before I opened my eyes, only that it felt like I'd run ten laps around the lake without stopping for a breath.

Moving like an old man, I went about cleaning up the mess I'd made. When I'd finished, I went to take a shower, still waiting for Leeson to ring with an update. He'd taken my insurance details and credit card with him in order to sort everything out for Vic.

Clean, and dressed in sweats and a loose-fitting T-shirt, I sat on the edge of the sofa, the array of pillows gracing it catching my eye. There were several of them, all brightly colored. Leeson had bought them because he'd said I needed some brightness in my life. The only illumination I needed was him.

I got up and wandered around what had once been a rather bland, impersonal space, taking stock of the changes. There were knick-knacks scattered on the surfaces, a pile of books on the coffee table, and a throw Leeson used when he read and snuggled up next to me. He'd turned the space into a home. Into *our* home.

I blinked, swallowing past the ball that had become lodged in my throat. I already knew I loved him, but it had just struck me how much. The concept of him being my special person had been just that, a concept, until Vic had rocked up all broken and damaged. What if Davey had managed to break Leeson's spirt and I'd never gotten the chance to love him?

Stop that train of thought, right fucking now. You do not need that shit in your head. Leeson's fine and he loves you. Look around you. It's fucking obvious.

A rush of urgency ran through me and I jumped off the sofa and grabbed my car keys to head out the door. The need to see him, to check that he was indeed safe carried me straight to the hospital.

It was only as I was led to the room Vic had been taken to that my heart rate slowed down. Leeson let out a little squeal as I lifted him off the chair he'd been sitting on, hugging him to my chest and peppering his face with kisses. "I love you."

He giggled. "I know that. What's got into you?" he asked breathlessly, wrapping his legs around my waist and his arms around my neck so he could cling to me.

"I just needed to tell you." It sounded lame, but with him in my arms I didn't give a fuck.

"You can tell me that any time you like. I love hearing it. But you might want to put me down before…" He pressed his lower body more firmly against mine. "You know."

I choked out a laugh that sounded more like a groan, Leeson's giggles returning. *God, I was doomed.*

23

Leeson

It took a lot of persuasion to convince Vic that it was okay for him to stay at the apartment, and that he wasn't kicking me out of my bedroom. Ollie was keeping out of everyone's way and not saying much. Given that Vic had only just been released from the hospital, I hadn't had a chance to check in with Ollie. I vowed to do that the first chance I got.

"Thanks for this," Vic said, settling himself on the sagging sofa.

"I don't need your thanks. I feel bad enough that I did nothing about Davey, and you ended up paying for it."

"We've talked about this. I made the choice to date him. I made the choice to stay after he hit me. Yes, he threatened me, but deep down I think I always knew they were fake, because I didn't really have anyone for him to hurt." He sniffed and wiped his eyes.

Careful not to jostle him, I sank down beside him. "Knowing it and doing something about it are two different things. I know that better than anyone. Davey has a way of sucking you in and making you believe his bullshit for a while. By then he's eroded your self-esteem and you start to believe the crap he spouts. At least you only put up with it for a year."

I was suckered into his bullshit for four years." That had been playing on my mind for the last few days. Did Garrett think I was weak for staying, for not getting out of an abusive relationship?

Ever since he'd torn into the hospital declaring how much he loved me, he'd been quiet. There was a lot going on behind those stormy blue eyes of his, but he wasn't letting on what it was. For a man that normally just let rip regardless of how the words came out, he was being very guarded, making it more than obvious that something was amiss.

The knowledge that he loved me kept me from thinking he was going to dump me, but there was this constant niggle in the back of my mind that something had changed between us, and I wasn't sure if I was going to like what it was.

Just fricking ask him what's wrong, and stop second guessing yourself.

"Has Garrett mentioned how much I owe him for the hospital stay?"

Vic's question pulled me from my thoughts. I glanced at him, his face not as swollen but still a rainbow of macabre colors. "I've told you, as has Garrett, stop worrying about the cost."

"I can't. I hate owing anyone money. It's not right. My Mom would turn in her grave if she knew that I hadn't paid back a debt."

Vic had no real family to speak of. His mom had died three years earlier, and he hadn't seen or heard from his dad in years. He had no siblings or any other relatives to speak of. He hadn't mentioned any friends and I hadn't pushed him on the subject because he'd gotten teary. "What kind of work are you used to doing?" An idea formed as I thought about Jen and Nese struggling in the store. "Garrett is going to need another store assistant when Jen finally leaves for LA."

Hope shone in his face, his lips tugging into a smile. "I've worked in a store before, though it was selling hardware."

"See, there you go. I'll have a word with Garrett and I'm sure he'll be happy to take you on. Then you can pay back your debt, have money for rent, and get your life back." I crossed my fingers, praying that I could convince Garrett that employing Vic would be a good thing.

Two hours later, I left Vic settled on the sofa with a fleece blanket, a drink, snacks, and the remote control for the TV. During my stroll to work, I considered how best to approach the subject of Garrett employing Vic. Should I speak to Jen first?

It had become apparent that with the increase in sales from the addition of my sweet creations, one person in the store wasn't going to be enough. And that was without taking into consideration the online orders, which were taking off too.

The date that Jen was supposed to leave for LA was looming. She'd planned to be gone after the Easter celebrations, and that was only about a week away.

"Hi Lee," came a shout from across the street.

It still surprised me that people spoke to me when small towns tended to take an age to accept new folks. Grinning, I gave Cez, one of the regulars from the store, a wave and kept going, knowing she'd want to gossip if

I stopped. Slowing as I approached the store, I started to count the number of customers queuing as I passed them. I nodded to some of the regulars as I headed into the store. Jen gave me a smile, but it didn't reach her eyes. What was wrong with her? Was she worried about leaving?

Even though it was my day off, I headed behind the counter to help, hoping it would give me an opportunity to find out what was going on with her and mention Vic. The morning soon turned into afternoon, and before I realized we were getting ready to close the doors. Garrett's idea of only being open from nine till two seemed to work, the store full most of the time.

As Jen went to pick up the empty trays to head into the kitchen, I lay my hand on her arm to stop her, glancing over at Nese. "Nese, can you take these into the kitchen while I have a word with Jen?"

"Yep, give them here." She reached out, Jen handing the trays to her.

Jen's brows arched but she waited until Nese had disappeared before she spoke. "What's up?"

"Do you think Garrett could be persuaded to take on Vic in the store?" I blurted out.

A spark of interest lit up Jen's face and she tapped her chin with one finger. "You noticed we needed someone else?"

"How could I not? The store is overflowing with customers. You and Nese haven't left before four o'clock in ages due to the extra online orders. Heck, if I wasn't helping Garrett make candy, I'm not sure he'd be able to keep up with the demand."

"The extra business isn't all Garrett's doing. It's down to you too. Folks can tell who made which candy, it's easy to see. Anyway, that doesn't matter. I take it you haven't mentioned this to Garrett yet?"

"No, I only thought about it today when Vic got out of the hospital. He's worked in a hardware store before so he'll be familiar with using a cash register, and selling is selling. I could tell him about the candy we make, and make him a crib sheet so that he knows the different kinds we offer." I warmed even further to the idea as I spoke.

"I think it could work, but I'd suggest him not starting until his face looks less colorful. He might scare off the customers."

"Yeah, but that means..." I trailed off, hating to point out the obvious.

"That I can't really leave town next week. I'd kind of resigned myself to that. My girlfriend, Shona in LA, has the rent deposit we needed so she should be fine until I get there. I've contacted the agency who signed me, and they'll give me a month longer but no more than that."

We'd talked a little about the job she'd landed at a casting agency, and her move to LA for it. It seemed that Jen had a talent for not only spotting people to work with her brother, but for all manner of things. Her best friend, Shona, had moved to LA a few months ago, and then persuaded Jen to apply to the same agency. They'd offered her a position at the beginning of the year with a start date of the beginning of April. That was why Jen had worked so hard to train first me, and then Nese.

With my mind racing with possibilities, I didn't question her further. "That's great, right? During the extra time you've got to relocate, I'm sure we could train Vic. I've got a good feeling about this."

"Yeah?" she glanced at the doorway which led into the kitchen. "We need to persuade big brother first. And he's been in a funny mood for days."

I sighed mournfully. "You noticed that too?"

"How could I not? He hasn't lost his temper once. I mean, that never happens, not ever."

"Do you think he's regretting asking me to move in with him?" It was the first thing that popped out of my mouth and resulted in a scowl appearing on Jen's face as she clipped my ear. "Hey, what was that for?" I rubbed my stinging ear.

"'Cause you were being silly."

"Okay, maybe so. But something is wrong with him."

"Wrong with who?" said Garrett from the doorway behind us.

Jen chuckled and gave me a "I'll leave this to you" look before walking past me.

Inhaling deeply, I stood a little straighter as I twisted round to face Garrett as he tagged on, "I didn't realize you were here. Why didn't you pop into the kitchen to say hello?"

I gave him my brightest smile as I moved to wrap my arms loosely around his waist. I tilted my head back to look up at him. "The queue was so long, I thought I'd just help out and then come and say hi, but it never got shorter." I rubbed at the center of his chest, a little disappointed that the cotton was too thick for me to be able to feel the springy hair beneath it. "I've been thinking. Nese is never going to be able to cope on her own once Jen has gone. You need another store assistant, someone to help fill the online orders. I counted this morning and there were over two hundred folks in here, and yesterday there were forty-seven online orders that needed shipping."

Garrett's expression gave nothing away as I laid out how busy we were. Not that he needed reminding when he was the one making the bulk of what was sold. "So, I was thinking. As Vic owes you money and needs a job to pay rent and buy food, that maybe he could come and work here?" I finished in a rush.

"I... really... no... I don't think that's a good idea." Garrett stumbled over his words as he moved back, my arms dropping to my side. I instantly felt cold from the loss.

He turned to face the store window, his back rigid and his hands fisted at his sides. Confused why he appeared so angry, I waited for him to say more.

"What about Davey? What if he turns up and finds you, finds Vic?" He swung back around, his expression revealing all the concern I'd heard in his voice. "I'll kill him if he so much as lays one hand on you. I would."

The sincerity in his threat left me shaking. I went over to Garrett on wobbly legs, unsure whether he'd welcome my touch as I stopped an arm's length away from him. "Is it too much? Do you want me to go?"

"What the fuck! Don't be stupid. I love you. Why the fuck would I want you to go anywhere. You only moved your damn stuff into the apartment a few days ago," he roared so loudly that I was sure the glass in the windows must have shook.

A smile spread over my face, my heart swelling in my chest. This was the Garrett who'd been missing for the last few days. This was the man I loved, the one who couldn't control his temper when he felt deeply enough about something. "I love you too."

That took the wind right out of his sails, his shoulders sagging as he leant his backside against the counter and opened his arms. "Then stop talking about leavin' me," he growled, hugging me tight as I stepped forward, as if he was scared I'd run off.

With my face mashed against his chest, I muttered, "Okay, as long as you keep being the big, grumpy bear that you are. I've missed you over the last few days."

He released a sigh which ruffled my hair before pressing a kiss to the top of my head. "I can't get the images of Vic out of my head. Then when I do, they're replaced with images of you, all battered, bruised, and broken. He could have—"

"Don't say it. Vic has reported him to the sheriff. They took pictures at the hospital and made a record of all the injuries he sustained. It seems Davey wasn't as clever this time at hiding his behavior. There was a witness to him beating Vic. When Vic rang to report the attack, they told him they'd been looking for him. Davey had already been arrested as they thought he might have murdered Vic." I chuckled wryly. "I hope he rots in jail."

"He's already in jail?"

I lifted my gaze to Garrett's. "He has been since Vic's disappearance. The sheriff was only too happy to report that when Vic spoke to him. The sheriff is coming to town to take Vic's statement and collect the clothing the hospital gathered in the next couple of days." I paused to lick my dry lips. "I've said I'll talk to him too. Is that alright?"

Deep furrows appeared around Garrett's eyes. "Why wouldn't it be alright? It's your choice. If you want to do this, I'll be there for you."

I worried my lower lip between my teeth. "I do want to do it. I was just worried that if it got out it might impact on your business."

"Get real. That won't stop folks from buying candy. The folks hereabouts love nothing more than something to gossip about. It's probably a good thing you're in the kitchen, otherwise you might not get anything done with people wanting to chat."

I could tell he was trying to allay my fears, and I loved him for it, but it could still have a negative impact on him and that was the last thing I wanted. "I'll make sure to stay out of the way." I sighed. "You're right. It might be for the best if you don't take on Vic—"

"Stop. I was more worried about you both being visible targets. It was never about not wanting to help Vic out. If Davey's in jail, then I'm more than happy to give Vic a trial run and see how he gets on. I've noticed how busy things have gotten, and that Nese was never going to cope alone. You've just given me a solution to my problem." He followed a wide grin with a swift kiss to my lips.

"Then you're welcome. And as we have a reward system thing going on between us, I think you should bring those lips back here," I requested.

Laughter rumbled through his chest as he shook his head. "Not a chance. I know your game, and people can see in through the window."

A wicked grin spread across my face. "Then maybe you should take me upstairs to *our home*. I'm not sure we've christened every room in the apartment yet."

He groaned, but I didn't miss the way his body had responded to my suggestion "You're a bad influence. You know that, right?"

"I think you mean I'm the best influence for a grumpy bear."

I found myself eyeball to eyeball with a grinning Garrett as he lifted me up. I wrapped my legs around his waist and threaded my fingers through the thick hair at the nape of his neck.

"A grumpy bear, is it?"

"Yes." I pressed my lips to his softly. "My grumpy bear," I whispered.

"Always."

One Year Later

Garrett

"Whose bright idea was it to extend into the vacant store next door?" I growled angrily to an unrepentant Leeson.

His fisted hands remained on his hips as he thrust his chin out at me. "Mine, and you know damn well it was." He pointed to the ungodly mess of the huge hole the contractor had made in the wall which separated the two stores. "However, I think you'll find it was you that told Timmy to take that particular wall out. Is it my fault that you didn't think of getting Vic and Nese to cover everything up before the men started this morning?" Leeson glanced around the store and shook his head.

Yesterday had been utter madness. We'd made a thousand Easter eggs in all shapes and sizes for the Easter Sunday parade the town had held. Children had come from miles around, Leeson seeing it as a way of celebrating the closing of the old business in style. And I'd let myself be talked into it.

After Leeson had advertised local handmade Easter gifts, the store had been packed with excited folks. It had been the same for all the events throughout the year. If there was a special day, Leeson insisted we celebrate it, and it had proven very profitable. It was the main reason we were expanding our business.

That was why we'd been woken by the sound of hammering. We'd dressed, eaten breakfast, and then excitedly come down to see what the men were up to. After Leeson had decided to enter the world confectionery awards, his talent in the kitchen had created a big stir. He'd created an exact replica of Sweet Haven's candy store, right down to full counters of candy. Each miniature candy was handcrafted and delicious. He'd surprised everyone when he'd won the top accolade for creativity and flavor. The controversy had come later when certain snobby asses discovered he'd had no formal training.

It had been one of the proudest moments of my life, and the reason why I wanted him to take this step of expansion with me. Yet, with a huge hole in the wall, dust plumes filling the store, and more banging and crashing, I was not a happy camper. Especially after Leeson distracting me last night had meant that I'd forgotten to mention to Vic that the men were going to be starting work this morning. The store had closed yesterday for an unforeseeable amount of time while the contractor carried out the renovations.

Last night, Leeson had produced his framed award and asked if he could hang it in the store, but I'd gotten distracted. *More like overwhelmed by the photo he wanted to hang up of the two of you.*

I swallowed a sigh, glancing over at the dirty picture frames. "You distracted me with your..." I shut up as I recalled exactly how I'd gotten side-tracked, my cock firming.

Leeson covered his mouth with the back of his hand to muffle his chuckle. Feeling aggrieved, I stomped toward him. He darted for the stairs to the apartment and I gave chase. As I reached the bottom of the stairs, his laughter floated down as he taunted me by wiggling his ass at me.

"If I catch you, I'll spank you."

His laughter grew louder as I got closer, but not close enough to get a grip on his T-shirt. He ran through the apartment door and headed straight for the bedroom, flinging his T-shirt in the air to land at my feet. Given that the store was shut, we'd decided to take a vacation, only here in the apartment with just the two of us having all the time in the world to do...

My brain lost its train of thought as I entered the bedroom to find Leeson naked, his cock hard and his slit wet with pre-cum.

He held up his hand to reveal a bottle of lube. We'd stopped using condoms months ago. A wicked smile appeared as he rasped out sexily, "My turn."

Any hope of ungluing my tongue from the roof of my mouth any time this century fled, as all the blood relocated to my already aching cock. It turned out that I enjoyed a cock in my ass as much as Leeson, and he was more than happy to accommodate me.

My hands shook as I tugged off my T-shirt and threw it on the floor before stripping off the rest of my clothes. Leeson licked his lips, making them gleam in the soft, morning light coming through the window. His eyes glittered with desire as they roamed over my body possessively.

In the past year, Leeson's confidence had grown with each new achievement he'd accomplished, such as standing up to Davey and confessing what he'd gone through. It had been a painful time for both of us, but it had been worth it when Davey had gotten his just desserts—a cell in the county jail for the foreseeable future. It had resulted in this cocky man who stood in front of me. He challenged me in ways I'd never dreamed possible when I'd walked away from my life in LA and come home to lick my wounds.

He'd enriched my life, taking away the pain of the past and showing me that there was more than just a passion for work. That passion hadn't diminished. It had grown as he'd shared his own love of confectionery with me. Together we were building something strong, and for once in my life it wasn't all about work, it was about love.

As I walked over to him my heart thudded against my ribs, my love for him huge inside me. "I love you."

A sexy sneer appeared as he threw the bottle of lube on the bed where it bounced once. "Then get that glorious, hairy body of yours on the bed."

His love of the hair on my body continued to mystify me. Teddy had never been a big fan, and had often complained that I should wax. I'd once suggested waxing my body to Leeson. He hadn't spoken to me for three days and I'd never mentioned it again.

I placed a knee on the mattress and slowly crawled toward the edge of the bed where he stood, my cock aroused, my balls heavy and firm with need for what was about to happen. On my knees, we were eye level. I reached for him, impatient for the feel of his naked body against mine. He came willingly, his mouth seeking mine for a kiss that was hard and commanding.

He licked at the seam of my lips, his tongue dipping into my mouth. He deepened the kiss and I lost myself in the taste of him. I moaned as his fingers slid into my hair and he held on tight.

Yearning beat through my veins as he released me and indicated I should lie on my front. Without any hesitation, I lay face down, grinding my hard shaft against the cover to gain some much-needed friction. Thankfully, I didn't have to wait long.

"Lift your hips for me," Leeson said. I did as he'd requested, moaning as he tugged my cock down between my spread thighs, his tongue tickling my slit. "So goddamn delicious." Hot breath ghosted over the head of my cock and I lifted a little higher, hoping he'd do more than tease me.

There was the sound of tutting and then the click of the lube bottle being opened. The wet tip of a finger slid down the crease of my ass. I swallowed hard and buried my face in the cover knowing what was coming.

"Don't you dare keep those delectable sounds to yourself," he rasped out as he plunged his finger deep in my ass.

"Jeezzzzz," I growled. The burn was immediate, but oh so welcome. I loved it rough, and Leeson loved to give me what I wanted, just as I did for him. I lifted my face from the covers and moaned like a ten-dollar hooker. "There, right there," I cried out as he crooked his finger and hit my prostate. My eyes clenched shut, pleasure mixing with pain as he added another lubed finger. He pumped hard and deep until I was humping the bed. "More, fuck, give it to me."

He sniggered, taking me at my word and adding a third, and then a fourth finger. My ass was crammed so full that he could barely move in and out smoothly, but it was everything I wanted. I rose up onto my knees, pushing back and rocking into his hand as he stilled to let me find my pleasure.

"That's it, ride my hand, and when you're ready I'll give you my cock. That's what you want, isn't it?"

"Fuck, I'm ready. Give it to me." Sweat dripped onto the cover in front of me and I held still as Leeson removed his fingers and changed position until I could feel the wet tip of his shaft against my slick hole. He didn't give me a chance to take a breath, thrusting into my loosened ass in one swift move. His groin hit my ass and I wailed, "Fuckkkkk, yeah."

He pressed his chest to my back, his lips fastened on my neck. "You want me to make you shout my name?"

"Oh, God yes," I answered unashamedly, grinding back on him and loving how full I felt with his cock buried deep inside me. The burn waned as pleasure took over. I felt so connected to him at the moment.

Leeson started off slow, pulling out only a fraction before pushing back in, the feelings merging with each other as his cock stroked inside me. "More, please." I rocked back, cool air brushing over my damp skin as his fingers dug into my hip bones to hold me firmly.

There were no more words as he thrust into me hard and fast. Flesh smacked against flesh, the sound only making my leaking cock throb harder with the need to come. My arms trembled with the effort to stay put as Leeson took me at my word and fucked me so hard that I was sure I'd feel him for days. It was perfect. Whatever doubts I might once have had about his size and strength had long since been fucked out of me. My man might look fragile, but he was a powerhouse.

My whole body was alive with need as Leeson reached under me to stroke my cock firmly in time to the brutal pace of his thrusts. I wasn't sure how long passed before I threw my head back and roared, cum drenching the cover. My ass clamped down on his cock as Leeson milked my cock. He growled, his hips and hand both losing coordination as heat flooded my ass.

His hips slowed, and he slumped over my back, releasing my limp cock from his grip. His slick chest stuck to my back as he gasped, "Give me five and then it's my turn."

I chuckled, my arms giving out. I collapsed exhausted on the bed, right in the wet patch. "Urgh."

Leeson didn't move off my back, his cock slipping free of my ass to add to the wetness beneath me, cum trickling out my ass and onto the bed. "We're making a mess," I complained without much heat.

"In Sweet Haven, something delicious comes from a mess," Leeson said, mimicking me and repeating something I'd once said to him when he'd complained about the mess I'd made.

My shoulders shook, Leeson rolling onto the bed next to me, looking sexy and dishevelled. I scooted closer to plant a kiss on his parted lips. "Then, it's a damn good job I hired you to help keep my *kitchen* in order."

"Is kitchen a euphemism for…" His eyes sparkled as he puckered his lips, leaving the sentence unfinished.

"Me." I murmured against his mouth, his chin tilting. I gave him what he wanted, what we both wanted, the morning sun filling the room as we both took the time to appreciate what we had together.

Sweet Haven might have been my bolthole, but Leeson had turned it into a happy ever after, and I couldn't wait to see what happened next.

Read on if you enjoyed, I've a new release coming in April 2021: Made to Submit, book three La Trattoria Di Amore Series. Find a snippet below.

MADE TO SUBMIT

Paulo

The scents and sounds of the busy kitchen faded into the background as Paulo watched with far too much interest as Carl's muscular back flex under the chef's white top he wore. Paulo bit at his tongue to prevent the moan from leaving his mouth. It was a close call. Only when his tongue was bleeding did he release it. Each day it became harder and harder not to give in and confess how he felt for the older man. Then again, Carl made everything hard...literally!

When pappa had said they were getting another trainee in the kitchen, Paulo hadn't paid much attention. Many people requested to come and work alongside his pappa. He was one of the top chefs in the whole of Italy and only offered to train those who were as dedicated to creating top Italian cuisine as he was. Massimo would never tolerate sub-standard food leaving his kitchen and those that worked with him soon learnt that the hard way.

His temper was renowned, and although Carl never looked all that happy to be bellowed at, he held his own and seemed to soak up every word pappa spoke. That level of concentration was a powerful draw to a boy who loved to cook as much as his pappa. The guy was a temptation and far too fascinating. Yet no matter what

Paulo did, he found himself gravitating back to wherever Carl was.

Carl had come to train and work alongside Massimo four months earlier, right around the time Paulo had come to some realisations about himself that left him confused and embarrassed whenever he got too close to Carl and found his cock misbehaving. He had taken to wearing tight underwear and baggy shorts to hide his problem when nothing worked to stop his body from reacting to Carl.

Carl's scent, and the way he looked in and out of his chef's clothing, left Paulo with wet dreams that made it impossible to look him in the eye most days.

"Vieni bambino, lascia Carl da solo al lavoro," Massimo bellowed from the other side of the busy kitchen. People paid him no mind, more than used to his shouts.

Carl was the only one who glanced up from the chopping board in front of him, a look of confusion on his face as he glanced between Paulo and Massimo.

Translating, Paulo blushed. "Pappa told me to leave you alone." His English was near perfect because of the amount of time he spent around English speaking people.

Carl's drool-worthy grin spread over his attractive face as he shook his head at Massimo. "Little P here isn't bothering me." He ran his hand over Paulo's curls and tugged on the end. "He's being helpful with teaching me Italian."

"Then he needs to teach you better if, after four months, he still needs to translate what I am saying." The words were butchered by Massimo's Italian accent.

Carl laughed. "Maybe I'm untrainable." He winked at Paulo, causing his fifteen-year-old heart to flutter madly against his ribs.

"Paulo, vieni qui."

Paulo's feet dragged over the red tiled floor towards his pappa, knowing without a doubt he was going to be shooed out of the busy kitchen. It had been the same every day after he returned from school. "Si, Papa?"

"Vai a fare i compiti e lascia Carl per andare avanti con il suo lavoro." As expected, his pappa told Paulo to get out of the kitchen and go do his homework. It was the last thing he wanted to do when Carl was right there to stare at.

Out of the spicy scented kitchen, Paulo headed outside into the hot sunshine. The heat scorched the top of his head as he ambled past the full restaurant, through the vineyard and up to his home. The house was a traditional Italian home that had three floors and all the bedrooms on the second and third floor had a balcony to overlook the vineyard. All the dark wooden shutters were open, indicating the cleaner was around somewhere.

The large patio area in front of the house, that held wrought iron seats and tables where the family ate at most of the year, with the exception of winter, was empty right then. Everyone would be busy at this time of the day, so he managed to escape up to his bedroom unnoticed to collapse on his single bed and stare up at the ceiling.

The sounds of the birds twittering in the trees and the buzzing insects came through the open shutters. His room was at the front of the house on the third floor, away from his parents' and Carl, who slept on the second floor. His older brother had long since left home and settled in Sorrento with his girlfriend.

Why did he have to be so young? Would Carl be interested in him if he were older?

He rolled his eyes at even contemplating that a man as gorgeous as Carl would be interested in him. His heart pinched as he turned to punch at his pillow before laying his cheek against the cool cotton, recalling what he'd seen the week prior.

Late in the evening Paulo had woken, wanting a drink. When he'd returned to his bedroom, he'd lain awake due to the heat. It was the sound of voices carrying through his open shutters that had drawn him from his bed and out onto the balcony. Carl and the other man must have thought they couldn't be seen in the shadows of the trees, but Paulo had seen them. He'd watched for too long, watched as they kissed and clung to each other, making noises that caused his body to react and sent him back to his bed feeling like a peeping tom.

Paulo had cursed his good fortune to find out Carl was gay, only to have his own hopes of there maybe being more between them in the future dashed by a stranger. More than a little upset at having his dreams crushed, he'd cried himself to sleep, but only after he'd dealt with his hard cock, imaging it was him that Carl had been kissing.

The all too familiar sensations travelled to his groin at thoughts of Carl's lips claiming his own and he ground down into the firm mattress, seeking something to relieve the growing need. It didn't take long before he found himself on the edge of coming, with his head and heart so full of the other man. It had been this way for months and there seemed little Paulo could do to change it.

Three minutes of grinding and stroking his shaft and his pants became a sticky mess. Breathless from shoving his head into the pillow to muffle the noises he'd been making, Paulo gasped, sucking in greedy breaths when he flopped onto his back. The warm sticky mess got him moving up off the bed and stripping. He eyed his underwear and the basket his mamma insisted he use for his laundry.

With a shake of his head, he dropped the pants to the floor and slipped on a fresh pair of shorts. About to head out into the hallway to rinse his underwear and hide the evidence, he paused when a familiar voice floated through his open window.

His feet padded silently over the tiled floor to the balcony. The sound of Carl's deep baritone caused a flush of heat to spread up his chest as he stopped just shy of the metal railing to eavesdrop.

"Yeah Nathan, this place is fucking unbelievable. Massimo is more than a little scary at times, but he's got some serious skills in the kitchen." There was laughter, followed by silence.

Paulo crept forward until he could see Carl's dark hair and powerful shoulders as he paced across the mosaic tiled floor beneath.

"Erm, not sure. I've scouted out a few of the local clubs, but nothing obvious here. The internet search for BDSM clubs came up empty too. Maybe you could ask about, see if anyone in the community has any ideas if there is something like that close by."

Whatever air had been in Paulo's chest left at speed, leaving him dizzy. He clutched at the warm metal balcony, his mouth drying at what Carl was talking about.

BDSM? Wasn't that some kinky shit? He wasn't completely dense, he and his friends had talked about sex stuff, but not this. Was Carl into something unnatural?

His spent cock seemed a little too keen on the idea and plumped. Paulo's heart flipped in his chest as he backed away as silently as he'd arrived. The dirty pants lay forgotten as he soundlessly closed the shutters to prevent hearing any more of the conversation, unsure his heart could cope with any more shocks right then.

His legs shook as he crossed the room and sank onto his bed, reaching for his phone. With a deep inhale, he opened the internet browser and entered BDSM into the search bar before he could think better of it. Imagines popped up on the screen and his heart immediately did a crazy dance against his ribs. Holy shit!

Picture after picture of men and women of all shapes and sizes appeared. They were in a multitude of different positions, some dressed in leather, others in nothing more than... well he wasn't quite sure what they were in but they didn't look comfortable that was for sure. Some looked more than a little ridiculous to his mind, but his eyes remained riveted to the screen. His thumb flicked at the screen until his mind was full of things he didn't understand, while his cock was deciding what it liked on its own.

By the time he put the phone down, his body was buzzing with feelings that left him more than a little anxious about what it all meant. His cock was painfully hard, but he wasn't sure which of the pictures had caused it. He stared at his tented shorts, his throat dry. Was he...kinky too?

His stomach quivered.

Was Carl a Dom or a submissive? Paulo dismissed the latter, sensing that there was nothing submissive about Carl, even if pappa could make the big man cower. Pappa had that effect on anyone who worked in his kitchen. Paulo had witnessed one of the kitchen hands piss himself when Massimo had chased the local butcher around the kitchen with a carving knife when he'd bought meat that was past it's best. The guy had never been stupid enough to make that mistake again.

Unable to sit any longer, Paulo stood and walked to the wall that held his mirror to stare at his reflection. His skin was full of pimples, his face a little too round, and his curls a little too long, making him look a little more girlie than he'd like. Would someone like Carl be interested in him? His young heart yearned at the possibility.

He stared into his own dark brown eyes and sighed, scowling at his own reflection before returning to his bed to pick up his phone.

Carl is never going to be interested in you! But he might if Paulo was into what he liked, too.

About the Author

Hi all,

My name is Jayne and I live in the Isle of Man. A tiny place in the Irish sea. It's an island steeped in folklore and history and just begs to have stories written about it, and one of my first inspirations. Over the last few years that has changed and now I find inspiration everywhere.

I'm an eclectic kinda girl so I've written contemporary and historical gay romance with a paranormal twist, daddy kink, fake boyfriends, out for you and enemies to lovers. My head is so full of ideas. I never know where it will take me next. I hope you have enjoyed this book, and if you are in need of more, then you can find all my other books, on Amazon and in KU.

If you're interested in keeping up to date with what I'm planning then why don't you follow and join me on the following links.

You can find me and follow me on:

Newsletter Sign up

Goodreads

Tumblr

Bookbub

Instagram

Twitter

Facebook

Website address

Facebook Author page

JP Manx Minx's

Patreon

If you would like to give me any feedback or just have any questions, go ahead and friend me on Facebook, and I would be happy to answer anything. Well, almost anything. I hope you enjoyed this book as it was a little different for me. If you would also like to leave a review, then I would love to read your thoughts.

Thank you for taking the time to be part of my dream.